"Why are you doing this?" K

"What?" He had the nerve to ~~~ m trying to be chiv~~~ the hostility betwee~

"There's nothing

The smirk on his ~~~ ~eve her. "We need to get s~~~ ~out of the way before we work together on this post office proposal and Felicia's wedding. All this tension between us is going to make Auntie Bren wonder."

"Stop calling her that," Kenzie started to squawk. Before she knew it, Ramon lowered his head and captured her lips with his.

Any sense of irritation or anger fell to the wayside. Kenzie pressed her hands against Ramon's broad chest. Her thumbs brushed against the buttons of his oxford shirt, tempting her to rip the material open. The familiar dance of their tongues excited her. Ramon broke the kiss and straightened to his full height. Kenzie wanted to smack him and kiss him at the same time.

"Good," he breathed. "I needed to get that out of the way~

Ma~ ~ng feel~ ~anted mo~

Dear Reader,

Grab your church fans, ladies and gentlemen, it's summertime in Southwood, Georgia. Wedding season is upon us—three weddings, a gala and a beauty pageant to be exact—and Kenzie Swayne doesn't have a date to a single event!

This small Southern town is celebrating its one hundred and fiftieth year—which is about the length of time Kenzie would prefer to have before dealing with Ramon Torres ever again. But being dateless has Kenzie sorely tempted to turn to the man who abruptly ended things with her last summer without a word.

You may have picked up on the behind-the-scenes chemistry between Ramon and Kenzie in *The Beauty and the CEO*. Their story needed to be told! In *Tempting the Beauty Queen*, Kenzie mentions her group of friends, the Tiara Squad, and I've got the rest of their stories for you, as well. Stay tuned!

Carolyn

TEMPTING
The BEAUTY
Queen

Carolyn Hector

HARLEQUIN® KIMANI™ ROMANCE

Recycling programs
for this product may
not exist in your area.

ISBN-13: 978-1-335-21672-4

Tempting the Beauty Queen

Copyright © 2018 by Carolyn Hall

For questions and comments about the quality of this book please contact us
at CustomerService@Harlequin.com.

H HARLEQUIN®

Printed in U.S.A.   ™ www.Harlequin.com

Having your story read out loud as a teen by your brother in Julia Child's voice might scare some folks from ever sharing their work. But **Carolyn Hector** rose above her fear. She currently resides in Tallahassee, Florida, where there is never a dull moment. School functions, politics, football, Southern charm and sizzling heat help fuel her knack for putting a romantic spin on everything she comes across. Find out what she's up to on Twitter, @Carolyn32303.

Books by Carolyn Hector

Harlequin Kimani Romance

The Magic of Mistletoe
The Bachelor and the Beauty Queen
His Southern Sweetheart
The Beauty and the CEO
A Tiara Under the Tree
Tempting the Beauty Queen

Visit the Author Profile page
at Harlequin.com for more titles.

I would like to dedicate this to Dr. Henry J. Hector III, aka my dad—The World's Best Father.

Acknowledgments

I would like to acknowledge all those in the pageant circuits—those on stage, in front of the stage and behind the curtains who come together to make their own Tiara Squad. They remind me of all the fabulous people at Harlequin Kimani Romance—the folks who can take someone like myself and make me sparkle. Thanks!

Chapter 1

"I was able to find a *Hamilton* ticket easier than trying to find a date for this month," said Kenzie Swayne, Southwood, Georgia's town historian. To say she had problems was the understatement of the century. Her strictly platonic go-to date, Rafael "Rafe" Gonzalez, bailed on her this morning. Something about the time being right to go after the woman he loved. Deep down inside, Kenzie knew she needed to be happy for her friend, but damn, couldn't love wait a month?

With a heavy sigh, Kenzie flipped her word-of-the-day calendar over. "*Lugubrious*," she announced. "Yep, gloomy, bummed and bleak pretty much summarizes my life right now." Where else could a girl get a hot guy who lived in the next town over to show up for important dates and who wasn't looking for long-term commitments?

At the hint of a chuckle, Kenzie glanced up at her dear friend, Lexi Pendergrass Reyes, who graciously hid her laughter behind her left hand, where her blindingly gorgeous wedding ring caught the fluorescent lights of the room. Kenzie grumbled and leaned back in her black leather office chair and rolled her eyes when the chair hit the wall behind her. Sure, her tiny headquarters in City Hall were small but she had bigger problems. She needed an escort for her cousin's wedding tomorrow and the four major events of June, when three friends were tying the knot, along with a gala and a beauty pageant.

"Come on now," encouraged Lexi. She shifted the four teal garment bags into her left hand and leaned against the door jamb. "What about one of the Crowne twins? Surely they're going to their brother's ceremony?"

The last wedding Kenzie agreed to attend and be in was a surprise for the bride. At least with Waverly Leverve, knowing about the nuptials meant she could at least back out of this one. Kenzie shook her head from side to side. The coppery, red-gold hair fell over her shoulders. She frowned as she twisted it up into a bun. She couldn't control her hair in this humid weather, so what made her think she'd be able to control her life?

Last winter Kenzie became fast friends with the handsome Crowne twins, Dario and Darren. They took Southwood by storm when they moved here to run their brother's garage. The single ladies in town were smitten with the twins and their playboy charm but alas, neither Dario nor Darren would work well as a believable date for her cousin's wedding tomorrow. Most of the Hairston clan, her mother's family, coming back to Southwood wouldn't believe Kenzie was involved in a relationship with either twin. Kenzie did not date playboys. Anymore. Playboys were a waste of time and she saw no need to be strung along by a man with a commitment phobia.

Four weeks. That was how long Kenzie was going to have to endure the scrutinous gaze of her kinfolk, especially Great-Auntie Brenda—Auntie Bren for short. She'd be there for Cousin Corie's wedding tomorrow, Felicia Ward's next week and the Southwood Sesquicentennial

Gala. In her mideighties, Auntie Bren was a force to be reckoned with. You'd never know her age by looking at her or witnessing her spunk. At her assisted living home in Miami, Florida, she kept friends like a queen held court. At the hundred-and-fifty-year celebration, more of Auntie Bren's friends would come and hear the story of her twenty-eight-year-old great-niece who was still not married or dating anyone serious. Both the Hairston and Swayne sides of Kenzie's family were attending and everyone would have a date but her.

"The twins offered to split two of the weddings, one with each, and the Southwood Sesquicentennial Gala and thought the three of us could attend Dominic's all together," said Kenzie, "but I can't. I need some*one, as in the same guy,* who will be here every weekend. Dario can do the first two but then he's swapping places with Darren. I think they're working on a project with Dominic, something about the baby's room."

"Aww," Lexi cooed.

"They look alike but not that much. You know Erin Hairston has an eagle eye. She came here last summer to help Chantal pack up for her big move overseas and had to point out to everyone in the studio how I had more freckles from being in the sun so much." Kenzie scowled and pressed her fingers against her freckle-covered face. As a child it was bad enough she sported this distinct red hair, but to top it off with more than a splash of freckles was downright cruel. Cousin Erin…*perfect* Cousin Erin, turned her nose up at beauty pageants to become an occupational therapist. In Auntie Bren's eyes, Erin was the closest thing to a doctor on the Hairston side of the family.

Lexi, gorgeous since the day she was born, rolled her eyes toward the barbaric florescent lights in the room. "Your freckles are what make you, you."

"Whatever. The least these spots can do is shield me when I'm dying of embarrassment when my eighty-five-year-old aunt is quizzing me about my sexuality."

As hard as she tried not to, Lexi laughed. "What? She wouldn't."

"She did with Maggie," Kenzie said of her older sister, Magnolia "Maggie" Swayne. "Auntie Bren started questioning her about whether or not she liked men and Maggie got graphic with the peach in her hand." Kenzie laughed along with Lexi. "So needless to say Maggie won't be seated at the family table."

"With any luck you won't be seated with Auntie Bren then," said a deep voice from behind Lexi. "I'm sure she put a hex on me."

One could hope, Kenzie thought before she realized who the deep voice belonged to at her door. The half laugh she almost shared with Lexi died and in its place came a scowl. By cruel fate, Kenzie's high school boyfriend, Alexander Ward, had been appointed city manager by his best friend, Mayor Anson Wilson. Kenzie was positive Anson had placed Alexander on the same City Hall floor just to annoy her since he held her responsible for not being able to get close to her friend Waverly. Last year Waverly Leverve came to town as a dethroned beauty queen being taunted by mocking memes of her crying when she'd had to give up the crown. Anson thought he could win her heart but Waverly was destined to be with someone better. "What do you want, Alexander?"

"Aw, babe, is that any way to talk to the higher-ups?"

Kenzie sneered and cut her eyes over at Lexi who made room for Alexander to stand in the doorway with her. "When the higher-up refers to me as *babe*, he reverts back to an ex-boyfriend."

Foolish as it sounded, Kenzie had accepted Alexander's marriage proposal at their high school graduation, caught off guard in front of hundreds of witnesses. She'd figured since they were both attending Florida A&M in the fall there'd be no problem. But the problem came when Alexander made several friends of the female kind over the summer semester. Kenzie didn't find out about his extracurricular activities until the first week she arrived on campus and was greeted by several other women who claimed Alexander as their boyfriend.

She'd returned to Southwood for a semester and endured a pity party from family and friends every turn she took. Not being able to take it, she'd left town for Georgia State and come back with her PhD in history. So far all she had done was archive the town's information to bring it into the digital world but Kenzie had been destined to be the first historian of her hometown. Southwood was in her blood and her family made history. The Swaynes, her daddy's side, and the Hairstons, on her mama's side, helped found the town a hundred and fifty years ago. So to come back to town after everything she'd been through, in Kenzie's mind, she'd had the bounce-back of the decade. In her family's eyes, she was twenty-eight and unmarried with no children.

Alexander doubled over with laughter. "She's still in love with me," he explained, giving Lexi a slight elbow to her ribs. Nobody loved Alexander more than Alexander. Everyone had had their role in school. Alexander had been president of their senior class, captain of the basketball team and shared the accolade of most likely to succeed with his best friend, the current mayor. Regardless of the morning's temperature starting off in the high eighties, Alexander wore a dark suit, including the jacket. The air conditioning these days was spotty, having to work overtime to fight the summer heat.

"Anyway, how are you doing, Mrs. Reyes? Ready to expand your studio?" Alexander went on to ask Lexi. "There's space right by your building."

"The building next door to Grits and Glam Studios, is next door to the old barber shop, and it's historic," Kenzie retorted and heard the contempt in her voice as she spoke. A hardware store had already disappeared when Lexi expanded her Grits and Glam Gowns to accommodate her successful pageant training studio.

"It's old, not historic," Alexander corrected. "The block of land belongs to the city, not the *Swaynes*, Kenzie. We're allowed to sell it to developers if we wish."

Kenzie cursed under her breath and shuffled through the stack of folders on her desk—her contribution to Southwood—and found the file she needed. "Here's the decree, marking the barbershop as a historic site. Martin Luther King Jr. had his hair cut here and spoke in front of the buildings in the sixties." The proof shut the city manager up and an awkward silence fell in the room. Both ladies waited for Alexander to leave. He lingered.

"Well, I'm good for now, Alexander," Lexi replied dismissively. "Thank you for the option."

Alexander ignored the dismissal. "What brings you to City Hall?"

When Lexi raised a questioning brow at Kenzie, Kenzie refrained from rolling her eyes.

"She's here to see me," Kenzie answered. "Is that okay with you?"

"You're allowed to have visitors," said Alexander. "It's kind of cramped in here. Would the two of you like to go into my office and talk? I have a beautiful view of the town square. It's beautiful this time of year."

"Yes, it is," Lexi answered, "but I just needed to drop off Waverly's dresses for all four events this month."

"Ah yes, starting with your cousin's wedding. I thought I saw Corie around town, or more importantly, her fiancé, Hawk Cameron."

Everyone who was anyone knew about Hawk Cameron, the star athlete for the Georgia Wolves basketball team. In the Hairston family, Hawk was more known as the man who'd knocked up the golden child of the HFG, the Hairston Financial Group. When Corie admitted her pregnancy, she'd been the topic of brief gossip. All seemed to be forgiven since Hawk stepped up as a father. *No*, Kenzie thought with a frown, since Hawk *the athlete* stepped up to the plate. Meanwhile, Kenzie was considered a pariah in her family's eyes.

"Was there anything you needed, Alexander?" Kenzie swallowed past the irritation growing in her throat.

Alexander admitted he had nothing and then said goodbye, leaving Kenzie and Lexi alone. Finally.

"Must be tough working with your ex?"

Kenzie frowned. "Not as bad as working with him as a boss."

"No chance he'd…"

Kenzie held her hand up to stop her old friend and mentor. "No, thanks. I'd rather run naked through Four Points Park at the height of mosquito season."

Mosquito season in the South was unlike anything else in the world. "I'll take that as a definite no."

"Exactly. I shouldn't be embarrassed or single-shamed just because I don't have a date, or a boyfriend, or anything to pass off as a boyfriend," said Kenzie.

"Hey, last summer you and…"

With a cut of her eyes Kenzie quieted Lexi once again. Days after the abrupt end to her summer fling with *him*, Kenzie had perfected the art of masking her hurt and frustration with spite and irritation. "Do not mention *his* name."

"Don't be so stubborn," Lexi joked. "I don't understand how you can work with Alexander but you can't with—" Lexi gave pause and consideration for saying the name "—*him*. You two *bonded* last summer."

Kenzie didn't miss the way Lexi's fingers bent into air quotes as she said bonded. "And then he humiliated me by standing me up for the party after the Miss Southwood Pageant. You know I hate to be embarrassed," said Kenzie. "And sure, I was mortified when I found out about Alexander cheating back when we were college freshmen. I could at least deal with Alexander when we started college, and thanks to a lot of therapy, I accept he's the one who should be ashamed, not me. Working with him, well, he annoys me but that's it. We have no…"

"Feelings for each other?" Lexi supplied.

An uncontrollable upper lip curl tugged at Kenzie's face. "Feelings?" She scoffed and waved off the notion. "Not a chance. I want nothing to do with *him*."

"That's why you had *his* truck towed?" Lexi mused and played along with Kenzie by not saying the name.

Feigning innocence, Kenzie batted her lashes. "Anyone who parks one inch too close to a fire hydrant needs to be reported, Lexi," explained Kenzie. "I was looking out for the good citizens of Southwood."

"Yeah, right," said Lexi with a knowing smile. "Well, look, let me get out of here."

The back of the black leather chair scraped against the pale gray wall behind Kenzie. It had a deep groove from the numerous times she'd done the exact same thing. "My goodness, let me get these off your hands." She reached for the garment bags and immediately the wave of guilt hit her. "I'm so wrong. Here you are, five months pregnant in the summertime. A woman in your condition shouldn't have to stand and listen to me complain."

Lexi waved off Kenzie's fret. "Trust me, I'd stand here and talk to you longer. I've been hunched over the sewing machine for the last few days getting ready for Bailey's pageant debut in a few weeks."

The two of them headed off to the elevators just outside Kenzie's door. Pressing the circular down button, Kenzie smiled fondly at the image of her seventeen-year-old niece winning Miss Southwood and keeping the Swayne beauty queen dynasty going. It meant a lot to Kenzie to know Lexi saw the beauty queen potential in Bailey. In the pageant world, Lexi was a goddess. Not only did a one-of-a-kind dress designed by Lexi bring good luck, but her guidance as a pageant coach always brought her girls in at least the top five of every competition.

For Kenzie's family, pageantry ran in their veins. So far six older relatives on Kenzie's father's side of the family were former beauty queens and four on the Hairston side, all before the age of eighteen. More had won Miss Southwood between the ages of nineteen and twenty-five, including Kenzie, but Bailey winning would be quite a feat for someone so young. Plus, there hadn't been a Swayne queen since Kenzie.

"I'm so excited." Kenzie beamed. "I know the former Miss Southwood is supposed to hand over the tiara but I plan on crowning her myself."

"Because we both know she'll win."

Kenzie gave her friend a high five and the elevator doors dinged and opened. As they waited, Lexi pressed on. "I can't wait."

After the elevator doors closed, Kenzie crossed the long hallway of her office floor toward the big bay windows to make sure Lexi made it safely down the front steps. Pride filled her heart at the sight of the well-manicured, lush green lawn of the town center. Cobblestone sidewalks encased the stretch of space in front of City Hall. Scattered diagonal parking spaces filled either side of the roads. Surrounding the area were diverse businesses such as The Cupcakery, Grits and Glam Gowns, The Scoop Ice Cream Parlor, Osborne Books and others in attractive brick buildings with colorful awnings.

Kenzie rolled her eyes at the only thing she considered an eyesore: the upscale Brutti Hotel, built last year. With its modern architecture and glassy windows, and height, it stuck out like a sore thumb amongst the quaint, old town setting. There was nothing historical about the forest area where the hotelier, Gianni Brutti, built the spot and it wasn't even considered Southwood land but everything about the place irritated Kenzie. The upscale hotel did push tourism, which kept revenue in town, so she guessed she couldn't be too mad. In the distance a church bell rang. She was reminded once again of her hectic month ahead. Stress over her single status was going to plague her. The second wedding would be worse only in the sense she would be forced to be around Alexander's and the questions from his well-wishing kin, wondering why the two of them never married. There weren't many things Kenzie disliked about her small town—the folks around here always remembered Kenzie and Alexander as a couple in high school but forgot about her heartbreak when she'd returned. His family, never knowing the full story, always felt the need to remind Kenzie that they were both still single.

In the reflection of the glass Kenzie spotted a sparkling strand of hair mixed with her awkward reddish mess. As if the stress of her life couldn't mount any higher, she'd spied a gray strand. Kenzie pressed her head against the cool glass to inspect. To make matters worse, she spotted the silver Ford F-150 truck driving down Main Street. The same tug on her upper lip returned, just as it had when Lexi almost said his name. *Ramon Torres was in town.*

There were a few things that could cause Ramon Torres to break the strict set of rules he lived by. After battling childhood obesity, Ramon had a no-sweets rule. But for the debut of the summer cupcake, the Wedded Bliss, sold at The Cupcakery in downtown Southwood, he made an exception. The cupcakes were so famously known and loved, Ramon took time away from his boutique hotel, Magnolia Palace, on the outskirts of town just to get one.

The other ban he broke was his No Kenzie rule. Southwood's historian had a knack for getting under Ramon's skin and under his covers. At the moment of spotting the unruly curly red hair secured in a high ponytail on Kenzie Swayne's head, Ramon Torres contemplated leaving The Cupcakery. Considering the debut of the dessert, he decided to stay.

What he hadn't planned on was the way his body responded to the sight of Kenzie's backside in a pair of light-colored jeans. She teetered on a pair of red heels and he recalled how her long legs felt wrapped around his waist. He then ticked off the Yankees' last world series starting lineup in his mind. If he planned on breaking a rule, let it at least be one, not two, in a single day.

The dozen people separating them weren't enough. He needed a battalion. Ramon shifted in his boots and tried to blend in with the group of high school–aged football players with letterman jackets. According to the time on his watch, school hadn't let out yet. Skipping class with identifying clothing to get a cupcake wasn't smart, but Ramon understood. A couple of bankers Ramon worked with on occasion waited patiently in line. Even the kids he'd seen hanging around in the park doing nothing but skateboarding and intimidating some of the locals stopped and stood in line for a cupcake. Ramon understood the things a person was willing to sacrifice for a cupcake. In his quest for one, he'd put himself in the path of the wrath of Kenzie.

Last summer had given Ramon and Kenzie the spark they'd needed to enjoy some heated moments together. Their time had been brief, but most of all pleasurable, until Ramon realized what a distraction Kenzie had been. He'd moved to Southwood to get away from his controlling family. Generation after generation, the Torres men and women were successful. Ramon knew how to throw a party. The family always teased him about making a "good time" a profession. His oldest brother, Julio, became the mayor of their hometown. Another brother became a United States Marshal and Raul, just one year older than Ramon, owned a booming nightclub in Villa San Juan. Ramon's own success gene did not kick in until he reached thirty and just as the gears started to grind, he met Kenzie Swayne. Kenzie put a whole new spin on sexy—and bossy at the same time. She'd been a dangerous distraction when he was supposed to get his life together and grow up. He couldn't live on his parents' property forever, so when the opportunity to buy the old, plantation-style home in Georgia came open, Ramon took it. Since he'd been so great at making sure his friends always had a good time, whether at a party or on vacation, Ramon turned that into a profession and opened the doors to the boutique hotel for families to come and enjoy the Southern town. Magnolia Palace was his baby, his investment and his chance to prove to his family he'd matured.

They worked together on a favorite pastime of Southwood's—the Miss Southwood Beauty Pageant—as a favor to his extended family. Lexi Pendergrass, a former beauty queen, had married Ramon's cousin Stephen. Stephen and his brother Nate were closer to Ramon than his own brothers. With Lexi being kin, as they said in Southwood, Ramon helped her out when the theater downtown, the usual beauty pageant venue, flooded by hosting it at his hotel, Magnolia Palace. With hindsight being 20/20, Ramon now knew he had been in no place to start anything. Had he known hosting the competition would get him involved with Kenzie, Ramon would never have done it. Kenzie wanted a man who was ready to settle down and Ramon was getting on his own two feet.

Ahead of him in line, Kenzie dropped something from her pocket when she retrieved her cell phone from her hip. The ample, heart-shaped view of her behind caused Ramon to forget about the No Kenzie rule. Every red-blooded male in line sighed and cocked their heads to the side to unabashedly appreciate the view. A collective sigh of admiration stretched through the store. Unaware, Kenzie straightened and juggled her oversize purse on her shoulder and committed the ultimate sin…she stepped aside. Whoever was on the other end must have been pretty damn important. Ramon's jaw twitched with a twinge of something. He couldn't put his finger on the feeling. He didn't like the idea of someone so important in her life.

"Torres," someone called out.

Ramon willed Mr. Myers to keep quiet until Kenzie left the bakery. The retired history teacher went so far as to wave his arms in the air. Ramon offered a quiet head nod in the direction where Mr. Myers sat with three older women. He breathed a sigh of relief when the glass doors closed behind Kenzie.

"Hey," Ramon said with a head nod in the direction of the table. The line moved forward to the point where the glass counter came into view. Ramon counted the number of people in line versus the number of cupcakes in the display case. If his calculations were correct and if everyone purchased only one cupcake, there would be two left by the time he reached the register.

"Get your stuff and come over here," Mr. Myers ordered. "I want you to meet my fiancée."

Fiancée? Ramon thought to himself. Which one? At seventy-eight, Mr. Myers had earned his reputation as a ladies' man, splitting his time between the two Southwood senior centers. Ramon pointed toward his watch and shook his head, praying the old man understood the silent apology. He didn't want to be here if Kenzie returned. Bad things happened when she was around. Once, and he couldn't prove it, Ramon had gone to sprinkle salt on his fries at the Food Truck Thursday event at Four Points Park and managed to get a snow mountain of salt. And even though he couldn't prove it, Ramon still felt Kenzie had something to do with his name being taken off the Christmas Advisory Council. Anyone with a business in Southwood wanted to be a part of the CAC. The council also helped bring cheer to town. He was also denied membership to a lot of Southwood events because his hotel was slightly outside of Southwood. Also last year, Ramon wanted to invite the whole town to his hotel for a holiday party but the email was somehow lost in the cyber world. And because the committee had gone for an old-fashioned theme last year, guess who had been in charge of all things last Christmas? None other than Kenzie Swayne.

Hell hath no fury like a woman stood up. Apparently Kenzie was the type of woman who didn't appreciate him bailing on her at the last pageant event last year. That was when Ramon decided to keep his distance and work on a No Kenzie rule…meaning, if he knew she was going to attend the same function as him, Ramon stayed away. So far Ramon had managed not to bump into her face-to-face for six months now. Soon everything would change. Ramon planned on starting up a business not just in Southwood city limits but in the historic downtown area. He was going to get a seat at that damn Christmas Advisory Council this year.

As the cashier argued with a customer, Ramon spied the back of Kenzie's head leaving the park. The fact his body still reacted to the sight of her proved he needed the No Kenzie rule. Pavlov's classical conditioning theory went into effect and induced a mouthwatering reaction, much like at his mother's coquito cupcakes. He still craved her. Just like the desserts, Kenzie was bad for his health and bad for Ramon's concentration.

"All right, guys," announced Tiffani, the cashier behind the counter, "after this batch I'm out of the Wedded Bliss cupcakes. I'm shorthanded today, so I'll need to take a break and make up some more. It will be about an hour until they're ready."

Groans from the customers drowned out Ramon's curses. The line moved forward. Folks behind him left the line, uttering their decision to come back later. As calculated, everyone else in line bought their share of cupcakes, except for the high school students who left, probably due to class. By the time Ramon reached the display counter there were five cupcakes left and no one behind him.

"Looks like you're in luck," Tiffani gushed when she realized he was next. "I'll let you have the rest."

"The rest?" Ramon imagined himself eating every single cupcake and then imagined how far he'd have to run to work them off. "I really just want the one."

"But there's no one else in line and these are going to

go to waste once I break out the fresher ones," Tiffani said as she boxed up the items.

"I'll tell you what, if you'll put four in a to-go box and leave them for the next customer who walks in, I'll take the one and pay you for a dozen."

"Sounds like a deal to me."

Once Ramon got his cupcake to go, he turned around at the same time as Kenzie reentered the bakery. Damn, how much was this going to cost him?

Chapter 2

"You've got a lot of nerve, Ramon Torres," Kenzie hollered at his tailored suit. She hated the way her body heated up at the sight of the man. Ramon turned to face her. His broad shoulders slumped. And she even swore he rolled his neck from side to side, preparing himself for battle. The wind blowing between the buildings whipped a loose piece of hair from his annoyingly cute man-bun on top of his head. The man mixed sex appeal with bohemian chic and wrapped it up in a sharp midnight blue suit paired with black snakeskin cowboy boots.

"What did I do this time?" Ramon stopped his long stride in front of the old post office. He didn't bother trying to sound shocked to see her, which annoyed Kenzie even more.

"Tiffani told me you purchased these. I don't need you buying cupcakes for me," she told his backside as she approached.

"So don't eat them," Ramon responded.

Kenzie walked around his large frame to make sure Ramon saw the irritation across her face. If there was one thing that set her off, it was a man telling her what to do.

Kenzie had worked too hard for the last ten years to grow from a naive girl dependent on her boyfriend. But Ramon wasn't her boyfriend. No, he made it perfectly clear last summer he didn't want to be in a relationship with her. "Don't tell me what to do."

Ramon sighed heavily. "Do whatever you want."

"I ought to throw them away," Kenzie went on to antagonize him. These were cupcakes from *The Cupcakery*. No one ever threw them away, especially not out of spite. Besides, she'd already had a bite of the delectable lemony dessert when Tiffani informed her the previous customer paid it forward.

"You're not throwing anything away." Ramon called her bluff with a sarcastic laugh.

With the box in her hand, Kenzie crossed her arms. "Fine. But I just want you to know from here on out I don't want you buy me anything."

"For future reference, Kenzie, I paid it forward for the next person. How was I supposed to know you were going come back into the shop?"

Back? She took in his choice of words and hated the idea of Ramon having the upper hand. He saw her before she did? "So you saw me and didn't bother speaking? What are you, a stalker or something?"

The square jaw of his tightened. "You were on the phone."

Being reminded of the call infuriated her more. Alexander had tried to sneak a project by her without her knowledge. No wonder he'd been so friendly in her office. Had his secretary, Margaret, not given Kenzie the heads-up, Kenzie would have had no idea the old post office was being considered for purchase. "Whatever."

"Well, if we're done here…" said Ramon, taking a step toward the closed doors of the old post office. In two long strides, Ramon entered, disappearing from Kenzie's fruitless rant. So what if the man wanted to do something nice for the next person? But why did it have to be her?

The wind picked up on the street, blowing the unsecured hair from Kenzie's ponytail into her face. With a sigh she set the box of cupcakes on the top step and twisted her hair into a bun. The doors closed behind Ramon and left her staring at her reflection from the mirrored doors. Growing up she'd hated her naturally frizzy red hair, but she hated her face full of freckles more. Now with a glimpse of herself, Kenzie smiled in appreciation. It took her a while but she found her unique look appealing and if she did say so herself, as she looked down at her attire…she looked pretty damn good today.

Common sense told her to head on back home. She'd already gotten her coveted debut cupcakes. Now she needed to get home and destress about seeing her family at the rehearsal dinner tonight. She wondered if there was someone on Craigslist she could hire…or was that illegal?

The clicking of the lion's head antique brass door knobs on the post office door reminded Kenzie of her nagging suspicions about the building. Alexander planned on meeting his potential client in a few minutes and Kenzie intended to be here. Funny how he didn't mention it earlier. She understood the position of a city manager needing to bring in business, but at what cost? Buildings in Southwood were historic. Some of them were built before the Civil War. And he'd scheduled a meeting, knowing she was taking the month of June. "Spiteful bastard," Kenzie mumbled to herself. Her ex had sworn he would not let their past interfere with working together when he was hired as city manager.

A car sounded off at the end of the street and a couple of high school kids in two different pickup trucks were mock sword fighting with each other. Idle hands, Kenzie thought with an exacerbated sigh. When the drivers spotted Kenzie they honked again and waved. More than likely they were up to something mischievous in the post office. Kids loved to run around in there, regardless of the danger signs. Speaking of which, Ramon didn't need to be in the building playing around, either. Kenzie reached down and picked up her box of cupcakes and headed inside. Ramon needed to leave.

"Ramon?" Kenzie called out his name. Her voice echoed off the empty walls. An old counter filled with dust split the center of the room. The inside windows were boarded up with old newspapers. Sun damage had destroyed the dates of when the papers were put up.

Footsteps sounded off down the hall just beyond the counter. From old pictures, Kenzie knew there was an elevator. The four-story building was also a playground on Halloween. Kids loved to tell ghost stories about using the elevators and getting stuck between floors, but there was no electricity in the building so Kenzie never believed them.

"Ramon." She said his name once more.

"Are you following me?" Ramon's voice sounded through the dark hallway.

"What are you doing in here?" She followed the sound of his baritone voice and swore his footsteps moved quicker and farther away. "Stop playing around in here."

She finally caught up with him. Sun leaked through the paled paper on the back windows and backlit him. Ramon stood in the elevator car, his back against the wall and his arms folded. He could have easily been a model in an ad for sexiness.

"What?" Ramon asked.

Kenzie placed her hands on her hips and stamped her foot. She hadn't meant to, but she did. "Get out of here."

"Are you going to make me?" Ramon offered a cocky half grin and stretched out his arms toward her.

In an attempt to back away, Kenzie slipped on her heels but caught herself in the elevator doors and kept herself from falling. Ramon didn't have the decency to hide his laugh. "You're a jerk."

"Thanks," he replied. "Why are you following me?"

"I am not," Kenzie said standing her ground. Her eyes caught the debris on the ground by her foot and as she glanced up the air in front of her began to snow. *Snow?* A loud rumble above her head sounded off. The moment she craned her neck upward something pulled on her blouse and her body was jerked forward into the elevator. Thunder was followed by a hail of ceiling tiles behind her. Ramon wrapped his arms around her body and turned his back to the falling debris.

Nestled against his chest, Kenzie stood still until the deafening sound stopped. She should have been frightened but she wasn't. With Ramon's arms secured around her frame she remained safe.

Ramon leaned backward and tipped her chin up. "Are you okay?"

Lost in his almond-shaped, dark brown eyes, Kenzie nodded her head. "I think so. What happened?"

"The avalanche was the floor collapsing just outside the doors."

Kenzie peered around his arms. The doors were closed. A light flickered but she didn't know how. The building had no electricity. Then she realized Ramon held his cell phone over her head. She blinked.

"We're trapped," she said rather than asked. The silence was proof. The doors were closed from the fall. They were safe from the falling debris but they were trapped. Kenzie peered again at the doors, which now, in her mind, seemed closer than before. Her eyes traveled up toward the ceiling of the elevator…the low ceiling, which grew lower by the second.

"Hey now," Ramon cooed, placing his hand on her backside. "Breathe with me."

"I am breathing."

"Your breathing is erratic," he pointed out, pressing his hand with the cell phone against her breast. "Your heart rate is accelerating."

"Don't flatter yourself," Kenzie said with a dry laugh. She pushed his warm hand away from her breast. Her nipples hardened with his touch. Amazing how her body could flip from a mild panic attack to sheer desire. Damn him. "I get claustrophobic sometimes."

"Sometimes?" Ramon chuckled.

"Yeah, well, just when I'm stressed and nearly lose my life," she snapped.

"You're welcome," he said.

"What?"

"I just pulled you from danger."

Kenzie backed away from him. The cool bar on the wall braced her backside. "And I am pretty sure you popped one of my buttons off my blouse."

Ramon held the light toward her chest to see. As if naked and exposed, Kenzie crossed her arms over her chest. "I'll let the second floor collapse on you."

"Technically the third floor."

"What?"

"Why would you walk into a building you know nothing about?" Kenzie shook her head back and forth. "Never mind, I don't want to know. You know, if you weren't such a baby and running from me every time you see me…"

"I don't run from you."

Kenzie scoffed at him for interrupting her. "Face it, Ramon. You're scared of a woman like me."

"I'm not afraid of you," Ramon clipped. "I have something to do in here."

"Like what?"

"I have a meeting with Alexander Ward."

Dread washed over her. Thank God for the darkness. Heat crept across her face. She was sure a red tint would cover her freckles right about now. "You're the one he wants to sell to?"

"If the price is right." Ramon sighed. "And if I can make sure I follow some rules."

So Alexander had listened to Kenzie's advice on restoring the old buildings. The fact didn't ease her irritation. "So you're just going to buy up every important building in my life."

"Here we go," groaned Ramon.

"Here we go nothing, Ramon." Kenzie bared her teeth in the dark. "You bought my family's historic home."

"I bought a business, Kenzie."

When she heard the tone of his voice Kenzie's hands went to her hips. "Are you mocking me?"

"No, I am stating a fact. I am a businessman. It goes with the territory and let's face it, you weren't in the position to buy the place."

Though his words were true, it didn't take the sting out of hearing them. It didn't take the threat of tears rimming her eyes when Maggie once pointed out that Kenzie didn't have…what was it she said? *A pot to piss in to buy the place.* Kenzie credited the plantation home for having sparked her love of history. She delved into the Swayne family tree and its contribution to Southwood. The Swayne family had lived there before the Civil War and harvested a pecan farm. Folklore said the family gave up the home in order to save the farm, which worked in their favor. To this day Swayne Pecans was the highest quality pecan seller in the States; it was passed on from generation to generation and still run today by her father, Mitchell Swayne, and his brothers. Technically she'd never lived in the house. No one from the Swayne side of the family had lived in the house for a hundred years. But that didn't stop Kenzie from believing the home would return to a Swayne one day, preferably her. And Ramon had the nerve to turn it into a boutique hotel. Granted, the property never looked better, but she'd never admit such a thing to Ramon.

"You're breathing heavy again." Ramon moved close to Kenzie's frame. Large hands pressed against her shoulders. "Take a seat, calm down."

"I'm not going to calm down. I don't have time for such luxuries, I've got a million things to do and prepare for and I don't need to be stuck in some dark elevator with the likes of you."

"The likes of me?" He flat-out mocked her with a hard laugh and an overexaggerated Southern drawl. The elevator shook a bit. Did the space between the walls get tighter?

Kenzie felt the floor beneath her against the back of her jeans as she sat down. She tucked her feet under her legs and adjusted her frame away from Ramon's when he got down beside her and wrapped his arm around her shoulder. He smelled wonderful, like lemon icing. Kenzie's stomach grumbled. What happened to her box? Did she drop it?

"What other things do you have to do? You can talk to me. Or have you forgotten we used to be friends?" Ramon asked her while his fingers rubbed the nape of her neck. Kenzie tilted her head against his shoulder. They'd been more than friends at one point. If she remembered correctly, this slick move with his hands toying with the hair at the nape of her neck had landed her in bed with him. Kenzie scooted away. "Tell me what's going on."

"I have three weddings to attend, and my baby cousin is getting married before me. Not only is one half of my family coming, I'm attending the wedding solo which means I'm going to spend several hours with the tilt-of-the-head-pity-look from them. Then I've got two weddings for my pageant girls and all of them are trying to set me up with their fiancés' groomsmen and I'm desperate to take them up on the offer because at this year's gala, I'm going to have my entire family in town, the Hairstons and the Swaynes."

"Not *the* Hairstons and *the* Swaynes." Ramon gasped dramatically before chuckling.

Kenzie elbowed him in the ribs and pressed her lips together to keep from smiling. "Shut up. You have no idea about family pressure."

"I don't?"

"No," said Kenzie. "And did I mention the Miss Southwood Pageant is at the end of the month this year?"

"Hmm. Has it already been a year? Seems like just yesterday you were walking through the doors at Magnolia Palace and barking out orders."

"You're not funny."

"Sorry, I feel like I should get you flowers or something."

"Why?"

"Because it's the anniversary of when we first met," said Ramon, no hint of mockery in his tone.

A shiver ran down Kenzie's spine. "And the celebration of the first time I'd been embarrassed in like a decade."

"By me not escorting you to the *final* party? Do you know how many parties and events we went to? You had something planned every day for a week."

"Well, after everything we went through…" Kenzie began clearing her throat. "If you weren't interested, you should have said so, set the guidelines, not leave me hanging to get myself to the restaurant."

"You're mad because I stood you up?" Ramon asked softly. Kenzie responded by rolling her eyes. "I didn't mean to hurt you, Kenzie."

"I'm not mad about just standing me up. If you weren't interested, you shouldn't have started things up with me and then stopped speaking to me. And don't try giving me a lame answer like, 'It's not you, it's me.'"

"What if that's true?"

"Whatever, Ramon."

"Seriously." Ramon reached to his side and found her hand. "I'd just finished the reconstruction on the hotel. I didn't need to get into a relationship at the time. I'd just opened the hotel and you were a distraction."

"A distraction?" Kenzie's bottom lip poked out. "Gee, thanks."

"You're taking that the wrong way," Ramon said. He gave her fingers a squeeze. "Kenzie, you are like your hair, fiery and spirited. I moved to Southwood to start my business, not get into a relationship. One night with you and I almost forgot everything I came here for."

"Yet you still slept with me."

"I am a man," Ramon answered, "an utterly weak man who succumbed to the most beautiful, irresistible, sexiest woman on earth."

And she was a woman, and the two of them together made such a pair in bed. Ramon was the first man able to coax out a primal desire from her. She wasn't sure she'd ever get it again but was glad and irritated at the same time for at least having experienced the pleasure once—

or half a dozen times. Kenzie licked her lips. The anger at him she felt disappeared. "Thank you for your apology."

"Wait a minute," said Ramon. "I didn't apologize."

"Yes, you did," Kenzie replied. She pushed their hands onto his thigh and let go, patting his muscular leg before letting go. "You meant to."

Ramon began to laugh. "What?" He patted Kenzie's leg and chuckled. "I accept your apology also."

Kenzie brushed his hand away. "For what?"

"For all your antics. I know you were the one behind loosening the salt shaker at that food truck at the park."

The image of Ramon's mountain of salt on top of his curly fries evoked a giggle. "I plead the Fifth." She pushed his hand away.

"See, I knew you were behind all the crappy things done to me. At least I tried to be nice to you with my antics."

"Are you going to admit to sending me magnolias this spring?"

"Why would I send you the first batch of flowers blooming this spring?" Humor flooded his tone. Their hand game stopped. Kenzie turned to face him in the dark. Without needing to see his face, she knew he was leaning close to her. She gulped. He'd remembered her favorite flower. Kenzie's lips throbbed at the idea of kissing him again. Her heart raced with the idea of anything intimate between them again. He was a drug to her and getting addicted to him was not good for her soul.

"Kenzie," Ramon said softly.

"Ramon... I..." Kenzie paused but she knew as she waited with her mouth open he was going to kiss her. Her world shook; her heart raced. And she swore her heart dropped.

"I think the elevator is about to fall." In one quick movement Ramon pulled Kenzie onto his lap.

That familiar feeling of being on a roller coaster just before it went down the hill washed over her. Kenzie's bottom lifted off Ramon's lap. Her heart dropped. Ramon cradled her in his arms and absorbed the fall for her, protecting her once again.

There'd been no thought for his safety during the fall. Ramon just knew if the elevator made it to the floor there'd be nothing to absorb the hit. His first instinct was to protect Kenzie. When the elevator dropped, the hydraulics miraculously kicked in and the bounce jarred the elevator doors open to the lower level. Ramon hadn't noticed the windows from the outside but the light spilled into the hallway where the doors opened.

"Okay, so this time I'm going to thank you," Kenzie said, wiping the gray dust and dirt off her face.

The sound of her voice filled him with pride. She was okay. Ramon helped her, using his thumbs against her cheekbones, wiping until he saw the freckles. Relief hit him. His heart ached at the fear of something happening to her under his watch. Aside from family, it felt odd to care about someone enough to feel responsible for them.

Most of the businesses in Southwood had commercial space on the first level and residential on the next floor or two. This was a common usage in old towns. No one wanted to live away from their businesses for security reasons. Ramon understood the terror small African-American towns felt when angry white neighbors sought to destroy their homes. Since then, there had been subdivisions in Southwood, but people still lived in these split-plan residences. Without the use of cell phones or any other modern technology a postman in the past never knew when he'd have to meet an incoming stagecoach with the US Postal Service or send a telegraph.

Focusing back on the woman in his lap, Ramon blinked. "Are you okay?"

"I'm fine." Kenzie's voice was weak but she tried to smile. "Just shaky."

"That's to be expected," he said, easing her off his lap, where the proof of desire grew. That old, familiar, lascivious feeling crept through his veins. Logic fought the uncontrollable rush of excitement and impulse to touch her again. "Let's get out of here before something else happens."

Kenzie stood first but used his shoulders to steady herself, not realizing her breasts were in his face. Given what just happened, Ramon knew this was not the right time to reach around for her hips and pull her back to him. This was how things worked when he was around Kenzie. She took all common sense out of the equation, just as she had last summer when he needed to concentrate on business.

Ramon cleared his throat. "Let's try to find a way out of here."

Once he reached full height Ramon brushed off the debris from his jacket and did the same to Kenzie's body. His hands smoothed over the soft contours of her hips and breasts. Again Ramon needed to mentally call out the starting lineup of the Yankees.

"Are you okay?" Kenzie asked him.

Ramon glanced down at his pants, afraid of what she was asking, but realized she meant after the elevator's fall. "Yeah, I'm good."

Despite the decrepit state of the building the ground floor wasn't in a state of disarray. Dust piled on either side of the hallways. A half dozen doors stood outside the elevator shaft and Ramon grabbed Kenzie's hand to help walk her through the threshold of the door he figured was the exit. A pile of ceiling tiles blocked them and they had to step over it. The red heels she wore were covered with gray dust and the fabric of her jeans was frayed at the knees.

If Ramon had to hold her hand the whole time, he was going to end up pressing her against the wall and kissing her senseless. They needed to get out of here. Alexander Ward should be here by now and Ramon didn't want the man to think he'd changed his mind about buying the place. It did need a lot of work but he couldn't beat the downtown location. "Wait here," he told Kenzie.

Ramon left Kenzie's side and jogged down the end of hall to the exit door. The silver bar wouldn't budge. Damn it. Guided by the glow of her cell phone, he hurried back to Kenzie. "It's locked."

"Still no service. We can check some of these old offices," Kenzie suggested, making her way to the first door. Ramon followed her inside to the empty space. The faded paper covering the glass offered light but not a view of people walking around outside. Since Ramon was taller, he started toward the window to peel off the paper but Kenzie did some cheerleading jump and tore off a corner, bringing the whole sheet down. Impressed with the move, Ramon clapped for her and she took a bow.

"Six years of middle and high school cheerleading," she breathed, "are finally paying off."

"Are you sure? You're breathing heavier, unless you're having another panic attack."

Kenzie's eyes widened and her face flushed a deep pink. "I'm older."

"Ancient," Ramon teased. He held his hand out for her to take. "Let's check another room—no one is out on the street here. Maybe we'll come across the stairs."

"I think the stairs are filled with furniture."

"Why do you think that?"

Kenzie moved out the door and explained. "When I

was in high school, kids loved coming here and running through the halls, especially during Halloween. This place is haunted."

"What?" Ramon scoffed and closed the door behind them.

"I'm serious. I heard some kids came out Halloween Eve and things would be rearranged from the last time. So they'd booby-trap the place with rearranged furniture and come back and things would be different the next day."

"Sounds like kids were playing tricks on each other if you ask me." Ramon imagined his older cousins doing the same thing to the younger group.

"Maybe, but I believe this place is haunted. I grew up hearing a story about the forties. My great-aunt came here and sent letters to her soldier boyfriend off in the war. She came here every day and mailed a letter. Her beau came back and married another woman from Peachville."

Southwood bordered three other cities—Peachville, Samaritan and Black Wolf Creek—and had become home of their first post office. Like Southwood, the other cities were founded by citizens tired of the Civil War. Union soldiers tore through South Georgia and burned old buildings and land. When Confederate soldiers came home to nothing, some left and some stayed. Those who stayed worked with the lasting people of the land, former slaves and Native Americans, and rebuilt each city. All three worked in unison into the next century. With so many single women writing to shipped off military men during wartime, this soldier had probably met another woman.

"I think your aunt's boyfriend was a player."

Kenzie stopped walking and pondered his statement. Her lips twisted to the side and finally she nodded. "I never thought about it like that. But your belief doesn't answer the question about the noises heard here. The theater next door flooded last summer, which is why we had to hold Miss Southwood at Magnolia Palace."

"So?"

"So the flood started from here. The water has been turned off for decades."

"I'm sure there's a logical explanation." They came to the next office. Kenzie took a step inside but Ramon held her back. "Let me inspect first in case there's a ghost."

"Okay," Kenzie sang skeptically. "But if there's a ghost demanding the blood of a virgin, you're out of luck."

His blood pulsed, as he knew firsthand Kenzie wasn't a virgin, then settled with a splash of jealousy. Sex with her was addicting and it took everything he had to keep his distance. Clearing his throat, he entered the room. The smell of mildew assaulted his senses. Like the previous room the windows were boarded up with paper. Ramon moved to take the paper down before Kenzie.

"We're looking out the back windows," he deduced. "Let's try a room facing the street."

"Makes sense," Kenzie surprisingly agreed. She turned and crossed the hall before he had a chance to exit the room and like before, did her cheerleading jump and tore down the papers. Bright light spilled into the room. Dust particles floated through the rays of sunshine. "Bingo!" She banged on the windowpane. Her red-tipped nails sounded off in a rhythmic beat and the hairs on the back of Ramon's neck rose. He recalled what those nails had done to his back.

Ramon cleared his throat again. Kenzie turned and faced him. "I think we need to hurry up and get you out of here. You sound like your throat is closing or something."

"Or something," Ramon agreed. Sweat began to form under his arms. He took the jacket off and laid it on the desk once he entered the musty room. "Do you see Alexander out there?"

Her hand paused in midair, about to knock on the window, Kenzie turned to face him with a scowl on her face. "I'd rather he not be the one to rescue us."

"History between you two?" Ramon inquired before holding his hand up and swallowing down his first bitter pill of jealousy. "On second thought, this is a small town. Everyone has dated everyone else at one point."

"I don't want Alexander to know I'm here. He purposely didn't tell me about selling the place."

Ramon wiped his finger against the dusty, cluttered desk. "Not too sure I want to buy the place after all. Seems like a lot of work."

"Plus you need to make sure you maintain the history of the place," she reminded him with a sweet grin.

"Oh yes, that it's haunted."

The sweet grin disappeared and Kenzie shook her head from side to side. The button Kenzie swore he'd ripped off had indeed disappeared and he was left with a view of her lacy white bra. Ramon swallowed hard and tried not to stare at the swell of her breasts. Dust flew from her curly hair. Her bun was now loose and her curls dangled.

"Laugh all you want. Try spending the night here."

"I have several bedrooms at my hotel to choose from," Ramon said.

Kenzie rolled her eyes. "Yes, I am well aware." She took a step back and craned her neck for a better view out the window. "Let me get on your shoulders."

The idea of Kenzie's legs wrapped around his shoulders did something to him. "No."

"C'mon, I'm not that heavy."

Ramon rubbed his hands together and licked his lips. "As much as I like your legs wrapped around me, I don't think doing it now that we're friends again is a wise idea."

Getting the hint, Kenzie pulled her blouse together. "Oh."

"I'll check." He moved closer into the room and peered out the dirty glass. "There are more people." Like Kenzie had done a few moments ago, he banged on the glass. Behind him his companion began pushing the desk against the wall. Before he had a chance to question her, she kicked her feet out of her heels and climbed on top of the desk. Ramon glanced down at the legs of the furniture wobbling. "That's not safe—get down from there."

"The two of us banging together will make more noise."

Ramon paused at her statement. How could being trapped in a building be so erotic? "Kenzie."

"Hey! Hey!" she screamed at the window.

The jiggling of her body made the desk move more. Ramon wrapped his arms around her waist and pulled her off the top. She kicked the top drawer by accident and the compartment fell down, causing old papers to fall to the dust covered ground. Like a child on Christmas morning, Kenzie squealed in delight and shimmied out of Ramon's eyes. "Oh my God, what's this?"

"Old papers," Ramon answered. He knelt beside her and as she whipped her hair off her neck he whiffed the sweet, magnolia scented products in her hair.

"But what kind? Look here," she said, lifting up what looked like a legal document stapled to a blue construction-like paper. "Bank papers? Deeds? Oh, look." Kenzie scrambled around the floor and found a brass key. "What do you think this is for?"

Ramon inspected it. "It's too big for a desk drawer." He stood up, went to the office door to close it, where he found a closet. "Throw me the key." She did, but it landed on the floor halfway between them.

"I was a cheerleader, not a quarterback."

Grumbling, Ramon retrieved the key. The lock turned but the door wouldn't open. Humidity often caused wood to swell. Kenzie was already behind him when he shouldered the closet open. Musty air hit their noses.

"Son of a bitch," Kenzie said from between gritted teeth. "Someone has been in here and tried putting in an air-conditioning unit."

Ramon followed Kenzie's glare up to the ceiling of the closet. A silver-coated pipe hung from the top tiles. Rust-colored water stained the walls and the floor. Ramon would rather leave the belongings inside and return with a face mask but Kenzie had already started dragging the plastic bags out. She grunted and tugged at the top bag, an old army-green duffel bag. Ramon took it from her hands and tossed it behind them with ease. The next bags, oddly shaped, weren't as heavy. Kenzie pulled a picture frame from the top bag.

"The date," Kenzie breathed. "This photograph was taken over a hundred years ago." She pressed her finger at the date on the corner of the faded, yellowed newspaper clipping. Ramon wondered if she'd paid attention to the picture first. The image in the article was of a sheriff and his men standing over a body. The sheriff held a most wanted sketch and his deputy held up a picture of a newspaper. The fold of a paper obscured the names tagged in the photo.

"I need to look these names up, of course," said Kenzie. "What else is in here?"

They found more photographs, including some of the post office they stood in when it was first built. The streets were filled with mud. Instead of a sidewalk there were boardwalks. Mud tarnished the hems of the proud women's dresses. A box contained old, loose black-and-white photographs from weddings and men dressed up in military garb standing in front of an old bus, being shipped off to war. Another framed photograph showed the original structure of the schoolhouse.

"Before Southwood High and Southwood Middle," Kenzie began, "everyone was taught in the one school. Now it's used as a shed by the elementary school."

"I remember my folks talking about being taught in one school back in Villa San Juan." Ramon had grown up in a Florida island town so small, they'd only needed one for a long time. He realized Southwood and Villa San Juan weren't so different.

"It wasn't until the late fifties the little school had enough students and funding for a total of three brick and mortar buildings. After the Second World War, while African-Americans from other towns were coming back to the same segregation they'd left, Southwood's citizens banded together as they always had since the Civil War."

"Why don't you teach history?" Ramon inquired. "Didn't Mr. Myers retire?"

Kenzie pulled her hair up into a bun, exposing her long neck. "I wouldn't mind. I've substituted before. I can't possibly think about teaching right now. That's all I need my great-aunts and uncles to hear. I'm going to show up at these weddings and be labeled the spinster teacher. And now it looks like I've just hit the jackpot of artifacts. I can't wait to show all this off at the gala this month, providing the new buyer lets me keep them."

Ramon knew she meant him. He shrugged his shoulders. "I haven't decided yet. There is a lot of damage and I've got to keep up the historic regulations."

"True," she agreed, still rifling through the closet.

Ramon glanced around the room. The closet had now been turned inside out. In Kenzie's search, she tossed some things on top of the original bag. Small pieces of paper spilled out from a hole on the side.

"What's this?" he asked, picking up a square card.

"I have no idea," Kenzie said, inspecting it in his hand. "I can barely make out 'Southwood' at the top. Damn the water damage. I can't tell. What do you think it is?"

"My gut says an election ballot," he half teased her. "Maybe the current mayor didn't win."

"I wish." Kenzie frowned. "I hate Anson with a passion. Unfortunately, when he came along, we were doing electronic ballots. No, these look much older. Hmm, the mystery grows. I told you this place was haunted—you may want to rethink buying it."

"I don't believe for one minute it's haunted."

"You don't sound too sure." Kenzie poked his chest. "Scared?"

"I need to come up with a proposal for how I'm going to keep the historic features intact. Maybe I need a historian, someone who can help me with the Economic Development Council."

"Good luck," Kenzie huffed and folded her arms across her chest.

"Kenzie, c'mon, why don't you help me?"

"Why would I want to help you buy this place and turn it into something stupid like a hotel?"

"I already have a hotel. I can offer you something you don't have."

Chin jutted forward, Kenzie squared her shoulders. "What can you offer me?"

"If you'll help me with the proposal, I'll be your date for all your functions this month."

"No thanks," Kenzie quickly responded with a frown. The corners of Ramon's mouth turned upside down. "Oh come on," she breathed, "you don't think I would allow you the chance to stand me up again."

"We've moved beyond that, Kenzie."

"Oh sure," Kenzie said, rolling her eyes. "In a matter of minutes we've moved on. Whatever. Besides, anyone in town will know we hate each other."

"There's a thin line between…"

Kenzie stopped the following sentence from flowing by pressing her two fingers against his lips—that almost kissed her a few moments ago. The same lips that kissed her naked body on a bed of magnolia petals under the full moon.

"You know we can sell chemistry." Ramon wrapped his left hand around her fingers and kissed the tips.

Kenzie waited a beat or two before pulling away with a step backward. "How so?"

Ramon stepped forward and as if in a dance move, Kenzie backed up against the wall, right where he wanted her. He pressed his hands on the wall on either side of her head. Beneath her blouse her skin rippled with goose bumps. When he dipped his head lower toward hers she pressed her lips together and closed her eyes. Chuckling, Ramon caressed the side of her face.

"Because we can't deny it." His lips were practically on hers. He tasted the sweet lemon frosting on her breath.

"Mr. Torres, is that you?" someone yelled and banged on the outside glass.

Kenzie pressed her head against Ramon's chest and grabbed the lapels of his jacket while Ramon cursed in Spanish. "Think my offer over, sweetheart."

Chapter 3

"And what are you going to do?" Maggie Swayne asked, sitting with her legs crossed on Kenzie's pale pink cushioned couch. She grabbed a pink-and-gold-accented throw pillow and placed it in her lap, clearly desperate for more details of what had happened this afternoon.

Kenzie's traumatic episode this afternoon granted her an excuse to not attend Corie's rehearsal dinner tonight. With fifty Hairstons, Kenzie didn't think she'd be missed. Her mother, Paula, had already excused her. Maggie took the pardon to include herself, too. "Corie's wedding is tomorrow."

The big day had been circled on Kenzie's custom-made calendar on her stainless steel refrigerator in her downtown Southwood apartment. Each month featured a picture of a particular tiara Kenzie had won over the years propped up at one of her favorite historic places around town. This month's image was an old photograph of the Miss Southwood crown on a low branch of a blooming magnolia tree last summer. A year ago, when Kenzie took the job, glad to finally put her degree to use, she never thought it would be so unglamorous. She combed through old newspapers, donated family photo albums and yearbooks. Sometimes she went out in around town and took pictures of trees with sweetheart initials carved in the trunk. On one occasion Kenzie brought her well-earned tiaras along with her and made her own calendar. "I don't need to be reminded," Kenzie said from the kitchen entrance in a clipped tone.

"I mean, we can skip the rehearsal dinner tonight with no questions asked but Auntie Bren is going to have questions tomorrow for you."

"I like the way Mama excused *me* from attending and that includes you for everything but Auntie's wrath."

"Because the last time she got on FaceTime with me and asked where my boyfriend was, I reached over into the nightstand and showed her."

Auntie Bren had a habit of being on the stuffy side. Kenzie could only imagine the old woman's face.

"You're so crass." Kenzie shook her head at her sister, who poked her tongue out in response. "And I have answers for her," Kenzie said with a shrug. She joined her sister in the living room on the couch with two glasses of wine.

The windows were drawn open. The bright lights of the nearby amphitheater shone through, changing colors on the high ceiling. One of the perks of her apartment was the free concerts. She saw all the performances without ever having to leave her place. The downside was the noise level for the concerts she wouldn't have paid for nor taken free tickets to. Tonight's event included a young preteen pop singing group. Kenzie wasn't sure what was louder, the music or the screaming little girls in the audience.

Maggie took a loud slurp of her red wine before setting the glass down on the magazine-covered coffee table. "What are you going to say?"

"I'm going to tell her I worked my behind off at Georgia State until I received a PhD in Southern history two years ago, and becoming *Dr.* Mackenzie Swayne has occupied my time."

"Meanwhile your bed remains unoccupied," Maggie mumbled.

"Maggie," Kenzie gasped.

"What?" Maggie blinked her hazel eyes innocently. "I'm merely saying what she'll say."

"I'm not discussing my sex life with her because she won't bring it up."

Maggie snorted and reached for her glass. "Want to bet?" She cut her eyes over to Kenzie. Kenzie concentrated on swirling the beverage around in the glass. "Yeah, that's what I thought. So why won't you take this Ramon up on his offer? Hell, *moan* is in his damn name."

"Because being around Ramon makes me a different person," Kenzie answered honestly. "I was so mad at him I became bitter."

"But the two of you spoke today and worked things out. No one says you two have to sleep together. He needs help and so do you."

Sometimes Kenzie told her older sister too much. Granted, they were considered Irish twins, born nine months apart, but they bared all the features of twins. Kenzie was outgoing and loved to be around people. They favored each other in looks, with their reddish curly hair, although Maggie's maintained a better hold than Kenzie's. But Kenzie and Maggie were complete opposites. At eighteen Maggie couldn't wait to get out of Southwood. She'd planned on never coming back to live here and had almost lived up to her promise. The Swayne family fortune in pecans made it possible for the kids to never have to work. Kenzie and her brother chose to work for a living. It helped keep their parents out of their lives. Maggie opted not to.

Right now Maggie lived in Atlanta as a socialite living off her trust fund—her true calling in life. Coming back to Southwood was a step back for Maggie, yet when she did, she always scheduled a secluded, two-week break in the family's cabin in the woods over in Black Wolf Creek, away from her social connections in Southwood. Kenzie partly understood her sister's dilemma. Their last name was Swayne but everyone always asked them if they were Hairston girls. As a teen, Kenzie hated the reminder but going away to college, she missed the recognition. The red hair gave them away. Maggie's was lighter than Kenzie's and Maggie wasn't plagued with freckles.

"Maybe I'll tell him something next week for Felicia's wedding."

Maggie rolled her eyes. "I can't believe you're going."

"She was one part of the tiara squad."

"I'm not friends with the girls I competed with," said Maggie. "For Christ's sake, it's called a *competition*, not a friendship pageant. You almost lost your chance to be the last Swayne to ever win Miss Southwood."

"Felicia is always nice to me. When she found out her brother was moving back to town, she sent me a box of magnolias."

"You were banging her brother," Maggie pointed out, then shivered with a gagging noise. "Alexander was a creep then. He just wanted to date a beauty queen."

What Alexander wanted was none of Kenzie's concern. At least Maggie knew to drop the subject. Both girls glanced over at the curio cabinet filled with beauty pageant memorabilia. Maggie had her own set. The Swaynes were big on pageants, a tradition passed down from generation to generation. Their mother, Paula, met their father, Mitch, through a pageant, when Paula *allegedly* stole the tiara from his sister, Jody Swayne. Mitch had fallen in love immediately. The Swaynes didn't speak to their son the first year of their marriage.

Aunt Jody held on to her bitter loss for ten years and stayed away from Southwood. Aunt Jody attended family reunions but she vowed never to step foot at another Southwood pageant ever again. And she kept that promise, even when Maggie and Kenzie competed. Kenzie forgave Aunt Jody for not coming to her crowning and she secretly hoped she'd come back to Southwood, especially with the sesquicentennial gala right around the corner. With the one-hundred-and-fifty-year celebration one week away from the Miss Southwood pageant, Kenzie prayed Aunt Jody would stay.

"Can you believe Bailey is ready for her first pageant?" Kenzie asked. She reached for the photograph on her end table of the seventeen-year-old beauty.

"It's about time," Maggie said, throwing the pillow to the side and reaching for the picture in Kenzie's hands. "I love our brother dearly but Richard nearly tarnished the Swayne dynasty."

"Hairston-Swayne dynasty," Kenzie corrected. After their mother won her pageant, her relatives also tried out and won several if Swaynes weren't in the competition.

"There you go with your history."

Kenzie shrugged her shoulders and took another sip. "I can't help myself, it's in me."

"You could help it if *someone* was *in* you." Maggie laughed at her own joke while someone knocked on the door.

As if on cue, Kenzie's stomach growled. Setting her glass down on the coffee table, Kenzie smoothed her hands down the back of her green cotton shorts. Since she and Maggie weren't attending the rehearsal dinner tonight, there was no need to concern herself with the dozens of buttons on the back of the skintight black dress. The sexy dress lay across her bed, next to the outfit Kenzie planned on wearing tonight—her bathrobe. Kenzie's stomach growled again. She hadn't eaten since the cupcake earlier this morning. The box of desserts she'd left upstairs on the second floor of the post office had been lost in the rubble. Thankfully the pizza she'd ordered ten minutes ago came earlier than expected.

"What am I going to do with you?" Kenzie asked as she opened the door.

"Dressed like that, you can do anything to me you want," answered a deep baritone voice.

Kenzie realized she hadn't bothered peeping through the peephole. No one knocked on her door other than delivery men. "Ramon?"

"Ramon?" Maggie repeated, leaning off the couch so far to peer down the hall she fell over. Kenzie heard glass break and winced.

Ramon Torres stood before her, dressed in a black suit and crisp white shirt sans a tie. Gone was the manbun from earlier and now his hair hung loose around his neck. A lavender box protruded from his hands with The Cupcakery logo on the top. In his other arm he held a bouquet of flowers—daisies. *So he decided to pop up at my place with the wrong flowers?*

Kenzie rested her hip against the door frame to block him from entering. So many questions ran through her mind right then. How did he know where she lived? Last year their fling took place at Magnolia Palace, while she'd stayed for the week and where Ramon had never formally picked her up for a date. Why was he decked out on a Friday night? Why hadn't she cleaned her apartment? Kenzie hated having to clean. Considering she lived alone, one would think Kenzie could keep up with her own mess. Her project this week had been painstakingly combing through the old photo albums of Southwood High and scanning the pages to archive. But she chose sleeping in a few extra minutes over than tidying up every morning. Irritated with herself, Kenzie blew out a sigh. "Why are you here?"

The thick black brows hooding his eyes rose as if in question. Visibly taken aback by her annoyed voice, Ramon maneuvered his gifts under his arms and pressed his hands together to make the international sign for time-out. "I thought we moved on from the animosity."

Remembering how the afternoon went between them, Kenzie nodded her head and rolled her eyes. "Habit, sorry."

"No worries."

When Ramon flashed his million-watt smile Kenzie's insides felt all warm and fuzzy…something she did not need. "What brings you to my place?" It dawned on her Ramon might have come to the conclusion of her being in need of an escort tonight for the rehearsal dinner. "Oh, God, wait a minute. I hope you didn't get any ideas earlier. It's presumptuous to think I needed a date tonight."

"Whoa, I am about to go on a date but it's not with you," Ramon clarified.

Kenzie felt a draft of cold air sweep against her tongue as her mouth gaped open. "Oh."

To recover from her embarrassment Kenzie narrowed her eyes. "How are you going to propose taking me to all of my events when you're not available?"

"I am going on one date, Kenzie, not getting married."

To add insult to injury, Maggie cleared her throat as she shuffled down the hallway in time to witness Kenzie's embarrassment. "Are you getting some paper towels to clean up your mess?"

"That and I came over here to see who the sexy voice

belonged to," Maggie cooed and extended her hand as she approached. "Swayne. Charmed, I'm sure."

Kenzie cut her eyes at her sister. "The stain?"

"I am getting to it." Maggie said but she kept a firm grip in Ramon's hand.

"Maggie," Ramon said with a friendly smile. "Nice to meet you. How are you doing this evening?"

"I'm better now," Maggie flirted with a goofy smile.

Kenzie's grip on the doorknob tightened. Her other hand went to her hip. "The wine, Maggie."

"I was just heading to the kitchen," Maggie tried to explain but Kenzie pointed to the left, where her kitchen was. "It's over there."

Maggie's eyes widened. "She's bossy, isn't she?"

"No comment," replied Ramon.

"Maggie, go." Kenzie ordered her sister out of the way and stared at Ramon. "So what brings you to this side of town?"

"I realized I've been outside your building but never been in your place," Ramon began with a sly grin. Kenzie read his mind immediately. They'd slept together, several times, yet he'd never been to her apartment. Ramon cleared his throat. "I wanted to replace the cupcakes you bought today."

"Technically you bought them," Kenzie clarified and accepted the cupcakes. "But thank you just the same."

His large foot kicked a box into the doorway. "I also went back inside the post office and grabbed one of the boxes of old Southwood memorabilia you were fascinated with."

Excited, Kenzie knelt and squealed. "I can't wait to go through this stuff."

"I figured," said Ramon. "I'm also having those ballots reviewed."

"Cool," Kenzie breathed. "I love a good mystery. Maybe somewhere in this box is justification for keeping the post office as a historical site."

"Have you thought about my offer?"

Coming to her feet, Kenzie pressed her index finger against her chin to dramatically ponder his question. "Remind me again?"

Ramon shook his head from left to right. Dark strands of his hair spilled over his shoulder. "I know you know. You're struggling whether or not preserving the building is worth spending ten events with me."

"Ten?" Kenzie repeated.

"Three weddings mean three rehearsal dinners or at least receptions, along with the sesquicentennial gala and the pageant, right? Plus the times we need to spend together getting me up to speed."

Kenzie pressed her lips together. "What do you know?"

"I come from a large family myself, Kenzie."

"You never told me."

"Well, we never got around to talking when we were alone," Ramon declared with a wink and a lopsided smirk.

A feverish chill crept down her spine. Intimate moments flashed in her mind, of being tangled in the black cotton sheets of his bed. Kenzie cleared her throat and replaced the wanton thoughts with remembering how she'd sat at her window waiting for Ramon to show up and the humiliating way she'd smiled blankly at everyone at the after party who'd asked of his whereabouts or stated how they'd expected to see the two of them together that night.

"Either way," she said, finding her voice, "I appreciate your offer."

"But your pride and ego won't allow me to help you?" Ramon asked. "I'm not the same guy as last summer."

"Pride and ego?" Kenzie forced herself to scoff. It was easier than believing him.

Ramon nodded his head. His hair was loose around his shoulder and brushed back. The open collar made him sexier. *Damn him.* "Of having to tell me yes."

"Boy, you have her pegged, don't you?" Maggie laughed, coming back through the hallway with a roll of paper towels.

"Judas," Kenzie muttered and clutched the brass door-knob.

"Don't tell me you're going to cut your summer events short? Why aren't you dressed for the rehearsal dinner?" Ramon asked. "Isn't it standard for the close family to attend?"

"We're excused from going," Maggie called out, "on account of what happened today to us."

In question, Ramon turned and looked to Kenzie for an answer. She rolled her eyes. "She is piggybacking on the excuse."

"We're twins," said Maggie. "When you hurt, I hurt." She said it with such conviction Kenzie wanted to offer her sister an Oscar or Golden Globe Award.

"I didn't realize," said Ramon.

"We're not twins."

"We're Irish twins," said Maggie. "Close enough."

Ramon chuckled at the sibling banter. He'd mentioned he came from a big family; Kenzie wondered where he stood in the lineup. She pictured him as the overprotective big brother type—especially after the way he'd looked after her today.

"Well, thanks again for the replacement cupcakes," Kenzie said, wanting to end this bonding moment with Ramon.

"Have you given my offer any consideration?" Ramon asked.

"I'm good."

Ramon licked his lips and glanced down at her frame. "I know. But I asked if you needed an escort in exchange for helping me win the bid for the post office."

"As a historian invested in the community, I'll help," said Kenzie. "But I don't need help with finding a date. I am a well-rounded woman with a PhD and a beauty queen pedigree and tiara to match. I can handle a wedding with my family."

"So who were the cupcakes for?"

Ramon made it back to his cousin Stephen's house in the suburbs of Southwood with his sleepy niece, Philly. Technically Philly would be his second cousin because her father, Ken, was Ramon's first cousin. But given the age difference and how Ramon considered his Reyes cousins as brothers, Philly was his niece in his eyes.

"Uncle Ramon?" Kimber asked, turning down the booming music from her cell phone.

"What?"

"The cupcakes. Tiffani told me you bought a dozen just before closing."

There should be a baker confidentiality clause somewhere. Ramon chuckled and shook his head. "Shouldn't you be off somewhere backpacking through Europe like most college kids?"

"Don't change the subject on me," said Kimber, scrambling from her place on the couch in the family den. School books clunked to the floor. The kid amazed him so freaking much. Kimber lost her father four years ago. Her uncles, Stephen and Nate, had uprooted their real estate business from Atlanta to sleepy Southwood to move into their brother's family home and take care of Kimber and Philly. Of course his first cousins had had a few ups and downs trying to raise the girls but they all came out just fine. Stephen married and he and his wife, Lexi, lived at the home, raising Philly and their almost one-year-old son, Kenny. Kimber was home for the summer to help Lexi out with Kenny and wait for the arrival of the latest addition to the Reyes family.

"I didn't change the subject," Ramon said, "I just don't plan on having a conversation about my love life with my niece."

"A-ha!" Kimber exclaimed and pointed her finger at him. "So you admit to having a love life."

"Love life?" Nate Reyes repeated, coming down the hall from the kitchen. "Sex life maybe, but love? Never."

Nate was not known for his cooking skills and Ramon wondered if he needed to call the fire department or an ambulance for anyone who'd eaten his food. Thank God Philly and her sleepover gang ate breakfast at the hotel.

"There are children present." Ramon nodded his head in Kimber's direction.

Kimber glanced all around her with her hazel eyes. "Who, me? I'm grown. I am almost nineteen."

"We'll talk when you can buy me a drink." Ramon laughed.

"Hey Kimber," said Nate, "I couldn't find the sofrito in the freezer. There are like a dozen tubs of butter, though."

Ramon bent from the waist and hollered as Kimber headed out of the living room, grumbling about Nate burning down the house. "If that ain't Abuela's granddaughter, I don't know who is."

"Tell me about it," said Nate. "Her RA at school offered to switch dorm rooms with Kimber since her kitchenette is bigger so Kimber can cook more food."

"*Switch*, though, right?" Ramon clarified. "Last I checked, Kadeci Hall was coed."

When not living in Southwood and taking care of her family, Kimber spent her time at school as a linguistics major at Florida A&M down in Tallahassee. Ramon had helped her move into the dorm. Tallahassee wasn't too far away, just a few hours, but still far enough her uncles wouldn't be able to pop in on her. Being close but not too close was perfect for Ramon. Most of his siblings and parents lived in Villa San Juan, a small island city off the northwest coast of Florida. Even in Southwood, Ramon resided at Magnolia Palace, which was on the outskirts of town.

"*Switch,*" Nate emphasized with a nod. "So how did last night go with Philly and the girls?"

"Great. I used your advice and got a set of earplugs and everything was cool. Full disclosure though, we ate nothing but junk food." That reminded Ramon to give Jessilyn a bonus. Ramon had sent the hotel chef to the supermarket with his black card to get the girls anything they might want for their evening together. Jessilyn, anticipating the needs of preteen girls, made sure to have plenty of toppings for individualized pizzas and a boatload of ice cream sundae toppings, as well. "I didn't make the girls go to bed at any particular time, so I'm pretty sure Philly's tired."

"No problem. Thanks again for taking them."

"Any time. I love spending time with the girls," said Ramon. His newfound maturity and stability got Ramon to thinking about having kids one day. One day. "This was the best time to have them. The hotel officially opens back up for summer vacation today and we're booked solid."

"So you're going to be busy," Nate noted.

"Busy, but don't forget I have tickets to the monster

truck rally next month. We could never get one to come to VSJ."

"I know, right. Hey, speaking of monsters," Nate began. He took a seat on the edge of the blue plaid couch. "I heard you're going to put in a bid for the post office building downtown. The city council has been trying to sell off the block for a while now. Pretty big job to tackle along with the hotel. Why didn't you tell me? You know I'm your construction man."

"News travels fast." Ramon nodded and leaned against the arched door frame of the living room. "The hotel is in order and running itself."

"I notice you didn't say whether the news was good or bad."

Ramon shrugged his shoulders. "Depends on who you ask."

"What if I ask Kenzie Swayne?"

A pulse in his veins quickened. Ramon cleared his throat and raised his brows. "What?"

"Aw, don't 'What?' me, *primo*. News…good or bad… travels fast in Southwood. I heard the two of you were stuck in an elevator all night."

"I just brought back Philly from her sleepover at the Magnolia Palace, so we know the rumor is false."

"But you two got locked in an elevator?"

"We were able to get out after a while," Ramon answered, recalling the moment before the elevator dropped again. They'd almost kissed and he was pretty sure kissing fell under the No Kenzie ban. Of course now that they were friends… Ramon shook his head and cut off his inner monologue, only to find Nate staring at him with bewilderment in his green eyes. "Don't ask."

"I'm not going to ask a thing." Nate laughed. "But you

will have to excuse me for staring. I've never seen you so taken with one chick in my life."

"I'm not taken."

"*Smitten*, as Amelia would say." Last year Nate took himself off the perpetual bachelor list by marrying Amelia Marlow, a local from Southwood who'd tried hard not to return to town. Now she ran her family's ice cream parlor and supplied Magnolia Palace with fresh homemade treats.

Ramon pushed off from the wall. "You're just as bad as Kimber. I'm out of here."

"Wait," Nate said, coming to his feet. "What are you doing later today?"

Even though Kenzie turned him down for the offer to escort her to her cousin's wedding, a niggling feeling bothered him all morning long. "I'm not sure. What's up?"

"Stephen and I were thinking about playing some basketball later before it gets dark and the mosquitos come out."

So they weren't planning on going out at all? South Georgia was known for its flying pests in the summer. "I may have plans."

"Doing who?"

Ramon shook his head. "Don't try to live vicariously through me since you decided to get married."

Nate held his ring finger in the air. The gold band caught the fluorescent light from the foyer. "Don't knock it 'til you try it."

With a shiver, Ramon said, "I'll pass."

"So where might you be going this evening?"

"Funny you should ask." Ramon chuckled. "I think I may attend a wedding."

Kenzie took a deep breath, regretting the fact she had let her Uber driver leave. Folks were still entering the church, which she found a blessing. She could literally disguise herself as a regular guest. Walking shoulder to shoulder with a young female guest, Kenzie walked through the stained glass doors. The party she strolled in with parted but not before a baby in the arms of its mother began to wail. Everyone seated in the pews turned to see the commotion. Kenzie stood stock still. In the first five rows all of the bride's side of the family turned and beamed their gazes down at lonesome Kenzie. The redheads stuck out the most with their empathetic smiles, all of them surely thinking she couldn't get a date or keep a man. Aunt Shelly once asked Kenzie why she couldn't keep a man. This was the same woman who kept a man…or different men…in constant rotation—nonetheless, Kenzie tried to smile at the staring group. She even offered a shy wave. The strapless lavender summer dress failed to keep her from feeling exposed. Heat crept from her ears and along her jawline and she knew it split in two directions…up to her cheeks and down her neck. She cursed at her choice of clothing.

Perfect Erin Hairston, born the same year as Kenzie, hiked up the hem of her dress and made her way toward the front of the church. She was Great-Grandma Bren's favorite out of this generation of Hairstons. Erin was not only beautiful, with her sleek, chic, dark brunette pixie cut, but she was also smart, too, and looked down at beauty pageants. Kenzie tried to remind herself she was a gem, that she deserved respect from not only a man but from her family, as well. She was Dr. Kenzie Swayne, damn it. Despite all her credentials, Kenzie felt inadequate. Erin made fun of her so much when they were kids, Kenzie had this underlying complex when her cousin and family came around. This would be the point where Maggie would smack her up the back of her head and tell her to get over herself.

"Kenzie," Erin cooed halfway down the aisle. She waved at the guests in the pews, loud-whispering to a few of them about having to grab her little cousin who still lived in town. Kenzie rocked forward in her strappy summer sandals. The height fairy had skipped her when she was growing. Everyone Erin passed turned their heads in a ripple effect in Kenzie's direction. "You made it."

Was it too much to ask for the ground to open up and swallow her whole? Was it too late to duck back outside and take Ramon up on his offer? Seriously, all the man wanted was some insight on the historic building he wanted to purchase. Kenzie gritted her back teeth together, finally understanding the meaning of cutting off your nose to spite your face.

"And with a date no less." Erin's voice trailed off and her mouth spread into a bewildered smile.

At the same time as her chastising cousin spoke, a warm hand pressed against the small of Kenzie's back. Kenzie glanced to her right and craned her neck upward. Ramon, dressed in a black suit and a lavender paisley tie, glanced down with a wink.

"I didn't agree," Kenzie said in a low voice while gritting her teeth.

Ramon's warm breath pressed against the back of her ear. Anyone watching would have easily assumed the gesture was a kiss. "This one's a freebie."

Hell, at this point she was willing to do anything he needed.

Chapter 4

Twenty-four hours ago, Kenzie didn't think she'd be able
to hold her head high at Corie's wedding. She hated to
admit that even a few hours ago she'd almost turned around
and left the ceremony. *Thank God for Ramon.* Those were
words Kenzie thought she'd never think. But he'd come
through in a bind. It pleased Kenzie beyond reason to
watch Erin get all miffed. Sure, her cousin tried to sweet-
talk her way with Kenzie, but deep down inside she knew
she couldn't trust a word coming out of Erin's mouth.

Thankfully Auntie Bren was too occupied at church
to pay attention to Kenzie and her faux love life. CJ, the
bride and groom's two-year-old son, had everyone eating
out of his hands. Kenzie smiled as she headed back to her
table with two champagne flutes. After her embarrassing
breakup with Alexander in college, Kenzie gave up trying
to plan a family. There were enough kids in Southwood
who filled Kenzie's life now. She loved helping out the
cheerleading squad and then of course she worked with a
lot of the toddlers at Grits and Glam Studios, the premier
training studio for budding beauty pageant queens.

"You appear to have a whole basketball team willing

to accompany you today," Ramon said, leaning close to Kenzie's ear as he rose from his seat to let out her chair.

Kenzie approached the back table where she and Ramon were seated for the reception. She didn't mind. In her opinion the farther away from the bridal table she was, the closer she was to the exit door. The basketball team Ramon spoke of was actually five grown men huddled together, leering over the single Hairston women. "Who, them?"

"Them—" Ramon chuckled "—as in the University of Tallahassee's former starting lineup."

"Those are Hawk's friends." A little tug of disgust lifted Kenzie's upper lip. One of the players had had the nerve to approach Kenzie at the open bar and ask if the carpet matched the drapes. "I never pegged you for a sports fanatic."

"Fan," corrected Ramon. "And not of them particularly. Their team beat my school so I have a bit of animosity built up toward them."

"Well, aren't you childish?" Kenzie cooed, pressing Ramon's forearm in jest.

Ramon covered her hand with his and grinned. "Do you want to bring up childish things?"

Rolling her eyes, Kenzie pulled her arm away and sat back in her seat. "We're not going there since we're new friends again."

"New friends?" Ramon questioned.

"Yeah." Kenzie offered Ramon a half smile. "You did save my butt earlier."

"Does this mean you're willing to help me with the project if I escort you to the rest of your events?" Ramon ran his index finger along her bare forearm. "No one would question a thing. There are enough guests from Southwood who can attest to seeing us around town last summer."

The touch evoked a set of goose bumps down her arm.

The memory gave a wave of whiplash. He pulled his hand away from her skin but the space still burned with fever. Too much champagne? Kenzie cleared her throat and pushed the stem of her drink away from her slice of double-layered white cake with the raspberry filling. She blinked in Ramon's direction. He did look good in his suit. That didn't even begin to describe Ramon.

"Yeah, that's because…" Kenzie let her train of thought die down. For a moment Kenzie had forgotten about the deal Ramon struck with her.

"Auntie Bren loves me."

Kenzie's mouth widened. "What? When did you meet her?" Kenzie had made painstaking efforts to keep Ramon away from her nosy family members. After the official "I do," sealed with a kiss, Kenzie took Ramon by the hand and led him out the side door of the downtown Presbyterian church. She waited in Ramon's truck with him and fiddled with a new layer of lipstick before they headed into the reception being held in the recreation annex of the church. The photographer had to finish taking pictures of the happy family at the altar. When a typical summer shower fell while the wedding party made its way across the lawn to the reception, Ramon drove Kenzie over to drop her off at the front door. When did he possibly have time to meet anyone? The minute she turned her back on him, he'd make himself a part of the family.

"Maggie introduced me when you went to speak to the bride."

Kenzie glanced over her shoulder and spotted Maggie dancing on the center floor with a few of the members of the starting lineup. As if awaiting the death glare, Maggie turned toward the table where they sat and shimmied her shoulders with her tongue hanging out. "She had no right."

"Why?" Ramon asked. "Your Auntie Bren seems nice. Why are you so worried about what she has to say?"

"Don't call her that."

"She asked me to," said Ramon.

Of course she would, Kenzie thought bitterly. Who could resist Ramon's charm? All the man had to do was smile and women were putty in his hands. Well, she'd be the first to resist him.

Ramon continued boasting about how Auntie Bren adored him. "She expects to see us together at the sesquicentennial gala in a few weeks."

"I did not agree to your deal."

"But you're going to now, right?" Ramon asked.

"You realize you're not the only one eyeing the spot."

Ramon sat back in his seat. His thick brows rose. "What?"

"Yep." Kenzie pressed her lips together. "So whatever you thought your buddy-buddy deal with Alexander was, he offered the same slimy offer to everyone."

"All right, all right."

"Tell me, what it is you want to do with the building?" There, Kenzie thought to herself, best to change to something safe. Yet as Ramon licked his lips while processing her question, she only thought of the moment before he kissed her in the elevator.

"Southwood needs a Caribbean restaurant." Ramon puffed out his chest with pride.

Kenzie felt the corners of her lips turn down. "I don't mind another restaurant but the post office has four floors."

"Five if you count the basement," Ramon said, wiggling his brows up and down. Kenzie inhaled deeply and shook her head.

"There's a Caribbean restaurant over in Samaritan,

owned by the Rodriguez family," she said. "They have a variety of items on their menu."

"Been on lots of dates there?" Ramon asked.

As a matter of fact, she had. She and Rafe ate there on several occasions. Despite this not being a date between her and Ramon, Kenzie did not want to think about another guy, especially not the one who supposedly bailed on her. Kenzie folded her arms across her chest. "Where did you take your date to eat last night?"

"We went back to my place," Ramon answered with a laugh as if remembering what a good time he'd had. "We got pretty dirty in the kitchen."

Kenzie refrained from rolling her eyes by biting her lip. What Ramon did and with whom he did it was none of her business. "Just the kitchen?"

"And the living room, but I wouldn't let anything happen elsewhere, you know, like in the bedrooms."

A bizarre streak of possessiveness washed over Kenzie... she just wasn't sure if it was for his house or the man. Silly for either. But just who did receive the flowers last night? Was it someone she knew? "Just the two rooms?" Kenzie asked, turning the corners of her lips downward. "You must be losing your stamina in your old age."

"Well, if you must know—"

Kenzie held her hand in the air to stop him. "Spare me the details," she said drolly, hoping to mask any shred of jealousy. "Back to the ideas of things to do with the building. The Economic Development Council is going to want to see a business that will bring tourists to our historic district. Southwood used to have a printing shop."

"I'm not a publisher," Ramon answered. "Sports bar? Each floor will have a different sporting event playing on a flat-screen TV."

"The Teagues over in Samaritan have the closest thing to a sports bar," Kenzie countered.

"Are you preserving Samaritan or Southwood?" Ramon asked.

"I'm just helping Southwood maintain its originality. It has retained the same structure and sleepy culture since it was founded. We don't need to compete with the other towns, just enhance what's here and what we need," Kenzie informed him. "What do you think of a tutoring center? The district wants to step up its testing in the fall and having a quiet place to study would be fantastic."

"Now I know where I know you from," said Erin, sliding into the empty seat on the other side of Ramon. Kenzie glared at her cousin for the interruption. Oblivious, Erin continued. "You're the dude who bought the old Swayne plantation, Magnolia Palace."

"Guilty," Ramon responded with a proud smile. "Have you seen the recent renovations online?"

Erin waved off his question with the back of her slim hand. "I only saw pictures of the old place when I spent the night at Kenzie's. It was broken-down then. I would love a personal tour to see what you've done with it."

Of course she would, Kenzie seethed. She didn't know why Erin's flirting with Ramon irked her. Whom Ramon did things with was no longer her concern. They were friends now and she'd be happy for him if he found love... just not with Erin.

"The doors open tomorrow for the summer."

"Oh man, that would be awesome," Erin cooed. "Don't you think, Kenzie? We can have a cousin day. I wanted to discuss some things with you."

"I've seen it already." At first Kenzie feared her words came out sounding possessive; when Ramon's face lit up with amusement and Erin clutched the pearls around her neck, Kenzie gave her head a light shake. "I mean, Ramon was kind enough to allow the Miss Southwood Pageant to be held in the theater on the property."

"That's right, the Swayne family tradition," said Erin. "Ramon, do you know a Swayne always wins when they enter? Well, except for when my dear Auntie Paula, Kenzie's mother, won?"

"Interesting." Ramon wrapped his arm around Kenzie's shoulder. "And you carried on the tradition?"

Kenzie took a deep breath and prepared a slew of words for her cousin. Erin's side of the family had always looked down on the Swaynes until they started winning. She leaned forward against the table but Ramon slipped his arm around her shoulder.

"Coming from a family of four successful brothers, you will understand why Magnolia Palace means so much to me."

Erin cocked her head to the side and smiled. "And where are you from?"

"Villa San Juan."

Snapping her fingers on one hand while slamming her French-manicured hand on the table, Erin laughed. "That's where I know you from—you're of the Torres family."

Ramon lifted his brows in Kenzie's direction. He'd mentioned his family's name before. She knew Stephen and Nate Reyes were his cousins. Ramon reached over and grabbed Kenzie's hand. "Let's dance."

Without protest, Kenzie followed Ramon. The fast music slowed and blended into a ballad. Ramon brought Kenzie up against his hard frame.

"Your family is interesting."

"And what about yours?" Kenzie allowed Ramon to settle his hand against her lower back. His right hand engulfed her left. For a moment she worried about her palms sweating. The heated dance floor was overcrowded with guests. At six-foot-three, Ramon towered over Kenzie by a foot.

"My family isn't here," said Ramon.

Pressed against his solid body, Kenzie gulped. "Why does it sound like your family is off-limits?"

"It's not. We're just here with yours."

"Fine," Kenzie huffed.

"Why don't you tell me about what you think I should do with the building?"

Immediately she answered, "A youth center."

Ramon pulled his head back. His thick eyebrows furred together with question. When he used to question her antics, he'd give her the same look. Kenzie gulped and tried to block out the image of them last summer. Suddenly her mouth went dry. She licked her lips.

"Why a youth center?" Ramon asked, spinning her around in his arms.

Grateful for the brief break of contact between their bodies, Kenzie tightened her grip on Ramon's hand. She needed to focus on the topic. "Did you not notice the trouble the kids around town get into?" Kenzie asked him. "Think about what they did in the abandoned building. They need a place to hang out."

"Hanging out doesn't generate money."

"Does everything have to be about money?" Kenzie asked.

"I bought Magnolia Palace," Ramon stated as if she didn't know. Of course she knew. He'd called upon her services last summer— or rather she'd offered up her services. Ramon had taken her advice then, but something in his eyes told her he wasn't going to be as accommodating this time around. "What part of that makes you think I'm not a businessman?"

Kenzie rolled her eyes. "Well, you asked me what I thought."

A warmth spread over her body. Ramon drew his fingertips along the edge of the fabric where her dress and her skin met. In an attempt to pull away, Kenzie pressed her hand against his chest. His heartbeat thundered against her palms. He nuzzled his mouth toward her earlobe. Heat rose from Kenzie's core. Her bottom lip trembled with anticipation of what might come next.

"What are you…?"

"Shh," his warm voice said against her collarbone. "Auntie Bren is watching us."

Like with every wedding, the time came for the bouquet toss. The timing was out of order from what Ramon had witnessed in the past, but the garter toss had to come first while the bride verified the single status of all her potential catchers. Kenzie became the first person Corie confirmed as single. The way everyone pointed the fact out amused Ramon, who stood back and watched the single ladies line up like a football team ready for battle on the field. Ramon held his tumbler of rum in his hand and rolled his finger along the glass. Coming from a family who built its island city on the backs of a rum refinery, Ramon considered himself a connoisseur of the alcohol. Not Torres rum, but not bad, either. Ramon tried to focus on the drink rather than the commotion.

The dude who caught the light blue garter held the material over his mouth to insinuate a sexual gesture. Somewhere in the mix of single women stood Kenzie. If she was standing there the way she had when she left his side, Ramon pictured her arms were folded against her chest with a scowl across her face. Ramon laughed to himself.

"Enjoying the party?"

Ramon turned to his left and reached out to shake the hand of a man he met earlier, Kenzie's father. "Indeed I am, Mr. Swayne."

"Please, call me Mitchell."

"All right, Mitchell," Ramon said, trying out the name. "How about you? Enjoying the wedding?"

Mitchell Swayne's light brown features pinched together. "The wedding is fine. The bouquet toss is my least favorite part."

"Oh, really?"

"Yeah, if one of my girls catches it," Mitchell said, "I'm going to pay out the nose."

"Fortunately just one woman will catch it," provided Ramon.

"Let's hope it's the one who would rather take her eye out with a hot poker than get married."

Ramon was willing to bet the hotel that the least likely to get married would be Maggie. Last summer Kenzie had started making future plans for the two of them. Back then he'd been in a foggy haze of Kenzie and almost saw himself falling for the commitment lifestyle. Generation after generation, members of the Torres family married the first person they fell in love with without ever testing the waters. Ramon grew up not wanting to sell himself short when it came to beautiful women. Besides, he sincerely doubted the happiness of his family members. He heard his parents argue all the time. Roman never wanted that for himself. If he couldn't get along with his significant other, it was time to bounce.

If she was anything like his sisters and cousins, Kenzie had probably been planning a dream wedding since middle school. Kenzie struck Ramon as a planner. He bet she scheduled everything down to when she woke up, what she ate and when she took a shower. *Mmm.* His thoughts trailed off with the idea of Kenzie naked in his shower. It was one activity they had not gotten around to sharing. Ramon inhaled deeply and remembered who he was standing next to.

Oblivious to Ramon's nefarious thoughts, Mitchell leaned forward on his dress shoes as his shoulders bobbed and weaved, swaying to the rhythm. Ramon glanced up in time to see a bouquet hit the overhead spotlight. The crowd of women—and Mitchell—gasped and waited on bated breath. Petals rained down on the well-dressed women. Ramon wondered what the protocol for him would be if Kenzie caught the bouquet. Photographs were taken of the bouquet catcher and the catcher of the garter belt. He cut his eyes toward the table of basketball players and scowled. Did he truly want a photograph of some dude with his hand up Kenzie's dress to exist in history in someone else's wedding album? Ramon's grip on the glass tightened and the sweet brown liquid sloshed around.

In the center of the onlookers, a half dozen redheads darted down to the dance floor and formed a huddle over white buds of baby's breath mixed with deep green oval leaves and stems. Thanks to his six-foot-three height, Ramon had a slight advantage over the scene.

"Oh God," Mitchell groaned.

Ramon felt like a rock had sunk in the pit of his stomach. Baffled, he darted his eyes between the garter holder, who now leered and sinuously rubbed his hands together, and the mysterious light arm holding the coveted bouquet. Raised Catholic, Ramon understood the power of prayer but couldn't for the life of him remember going to mass, confession or even saying a prayer. But somewhere deep inside he heard his own voice under his breath pray…beg…for the winner of the bouquet toss to be anyone but Kenzie. While he remained unsure about a future or marriage, the idea of

Kenzie being photographed with the guy who caught the garter didn't sit well with him, either, even if she challenged him all the time. Ramon held his breath for a beat before deciding he couldn't watch. He tossed back the drink until he saw the bottom of the tumbler. Through the clear glass came a blurry vision of a woman dressed in yellow and jumping for joy. Beside him Mitchell cursed. Ramon did a double-check—positive Kenzie wore a purple-colored dress.

"I'm next!" Maggie shouted.

Kenzie waltzed back over toward Ramon. Her face softened with a smile and a sigh of relief. "Squeaked by another one," she boasted.

"Thank you, peanut," said Mitchell, opening his arms to embrace his daughter.

"Wait." Ramon chuckled. "So you're *not* the daughter who wants the huge wedding?"

Kenzie and Mitchell looked at each other, then back at Ramon before playfully nudging each other as they cracked up with laughter. Ramon scratched the back of his head at their inside joke.

"There is no way I am getting married."

"Thus increasing her slice of her inheritance." Mitchell laughed.

As the two carried on the hysterics, Ramon wondered what bothered him more, the fact that Kenzie didn't plan on marrying…or the fact she no longer wanted a commitment from him. Hell, last summer Ramon needed to walk away from their budding relationship because he just knew she'd wanted more than what he could deliver, especially when he needed to focus on his business. Now to find out they were on the same page all along? Ramon scratched his chin, still bothered and oddly offended, and wondered if he proposed to her whether she would say no.

"Your glass looks empty," Mitchell said, bringing Ramon out of his funk.

"Don't forget to get us some champagne, Daddy."

Now alone with her, Ramon cleared his throat. "I've never met a woman who did not want to catch the bouquet."

"I didn't see you muscling your way to catch the garter," Kenzie countered.

Ramon nodded. "True, but I don't know anyone here."

"You knew the table of Hawk's friends."

"But no woman I'd want to be photographed with. Wait." He shook his head at the frown on Kenzie's face and the fact he'd started off like a jerk. "It wouldn't be fair to have a complete stranger in their album for the rest of their lives."

"Or at least until they divorce." Kenzie shrugged, casting a skeptical glance over her shoulder at the newlyweds on the dance floor, and folded her arms across her chest.

Ramon tried not to stare at the way her breasts swelled in her strapless gown. He cleared his throat. "You know, there was a moment in the sermon where you didn't have to hold your peace forever."

When Kenzie looked back over at him, she gave an overexaggerated eye roll. "It's not my place and we're not that close."

"*We*, as in you and your cousin aren't close? Or *we* as in you and I aren't close?"

Kenzie studied him for a moment before speaking. She rested her hands on her hips. "Both."

Pressing his lips together, Ramon feigned hurt. More people began to fill the dance floor for the next slow song. Ramon took Kenzie by the hand and led her to the center of the group. Despite their height difference, they were a perfect fit. He assumed the strappy heels she wore helped. Kenzie's small hand fit in his, her purple nails clamped down into his flesh. He looked down into her eyes and continued their conversation. "And here I thought we'd reached a new level."

"Oh, we did." Kenzie laughed and allowed him to lead them to the beat of the song. "Just not the level where I'm going to start sharing my feelings with you."

"This is going to make this month awkward for all our events."

At the key word—*our*—Kenzie's eyes widened. "What are you talking about? I never agreed to your deal."

"Yes, but now that your family's met me, don't you think it will be awkward if I don't escort you to the sesquicentennial gala?"

"What makes you think I'm going?"

Ramon dipped Kenzie backward. He caught her full weight in one arm. "You're the town historian and you're the emcee for the event."

Kenzie opened her mouth to protest.

"Auntie Bren already told me," Ramon said before setting her upright again. A strand of hair escaped her updo. Gently he reached out and tucked it behind her ear. "I know you don't want to disappoint her. She loves me and said she's looking forward to seeing me again. Did you know your entire family is staying in Southwood for the next two weeks? Had I known, I would have offered up a special at Magnolia Palace."

Kenzie's eyes narrowed on his throat. With the intensity behind her eyes Ramon wondered if he needed to be worried about his life.

"Again, let me remind you that I never agreed to your deal."

"But I'm already here. Did I mention your family loves me?"

"Half."

"Is that a challenge?" Ramon asked with one raised brow. "I am sure the other half of your family will love me just the same. I believe your father is fond of me." He enjoyed spotting the dimple in her cheeks when she tried not to laugh. They used to laugh together and then when they'd ended things...or he had...the only thing Ramon received from Kenzie was a scowl.

"I'm not challenging you to a thing," said Kenzie. "And don't think you showing up today means I need you for the other things."

"And prove Erin right if you show up stag next weekend at Felicia's wedding?" For once Ramon knew something Kenzie didn't. He smiled smugly and reveled in it.

After a moment of sheer surprise Kenzie closed her gaping mouth. Her throat bobbed as she found words to speak. "What do you know?"

"I know you're in a wedding next week and Erin will still be here," said Ramon. "While you're in the wedding party, she's a guest. She just RSVPed this morning."

"How long was I gone getting my drink?"

"Your cousins speak fast," Ramon replied.

"I am not sure which is worse," Kenzie said, licking her lips, "facing my cousin again or saying yes to you."

"One makes you feel bad and the other makes you feel good."

"Whatever. I am not in the wedding," Kenzie corrected him. Questions formed in his mind but she answered quickly. "I declined."

"Great, that's more time we get to spend together at your place, for a history lesson of Southwood, of course."

Kenzie's eyes widened and her cheeks got a light red tint. Whether she said yes or no, Ramon planned on being there for his new friend. It might make it easier for him to win his bid for the post office and become an acting member on the Christmas Advisory Council, and they would have to work together.

"Thank you again for coming to my rescue," Kenzie said as she and Ramon walked out of the reception hall. A half-moon filled the evening sky, dousing the flames from the day's burning sun. The moment Ramon rested his hand on the small of her back, she shivered.

"You're cold," Ramon stated and slipped off his jacket. "My vehicle's this way."

Stunned by his chivalry, Kenzie ran her hand along the lapels as he rested the garment across her shoulders. The inside of the jacket was still toasty from the heat of his body. Her soul oozed with warmth. "This summer weather is so moody. Hot one hour and a torrential downpour the next."

"I'll take the weather here over the weather in Villa San Juan," said Ramon.

"We get hit with every type of rain possible."

A set of keys jingled in his free hand while he guided her across the paved parking lot. Cars of all shapes and sizes and ages filled the vertical lines. Thanks to Crowne Restoration, a lot of locals were able to drive their classic cars. Kenzie scanned the parking lot for Ramon's truck.

"I'll have to remember to pick you up in my car next week," he said.

"Two cars," Kenzie said. "Aren't we fancy?"

"Or practical," Ramon replied. "I love my truck but it's a gas guzzler on the highway to Villa San Juan."

The mention of his hometown caused Kenzie to think of his family. It felt like he had been avoiding the subject earlier tonight. "How often do you get to see them?"

"I was there a few months ago," answered Ramon. "I took my cousin Philly to visit her grandparents."

Kenzie nodded, understanding the family dynamics. Technically Philly was his first cousin once removed. Her grandparents were Ramon's aunt and uncle. Lexi drew a diagram last summer of the Torres family tree. Ramon led her to the passenger's side and opened the door for her. She climbed inside. After closing it, Ramon jogged around to his side and slid in. Their shoulders brushed and Kenzie tried not to think about the desire pumping through her. This was a simple case of hero worship. Ramon had saved her from an evening of embarrassment.

"Have you ever been?" Ramon asked Kenzie. She blinked at the words. "To Villa San Juan?"

"Oh, um, no."

"It's nice." Ramon pulled his car out of the space and began traveling through town.

How did they end the evening with small talk? Kenzie cleared her throat. "Maybe I'll take a trip when it's not raining so much. Humidity is my enemy." To prove her point Kenzie tugged at a stray curl.

Ramon chuckled. "I'm not sure when it isn't going to be humid. It's right off the water."

"Sounds lovely."

"You'd really like it, considering how much you seem to love history. The town isn't very different from Southwood."

Kenzie settled in her seat, crossing her legs at the ankles. "Well, now I'm intrigued."

"And like you, I come from a long line of founders. The Torres family," he said.

While they drove through town Ramon told Kenzie about growing up. His great-great-great-grandfather had settled the Florida island and named it for his home in Puerto Rico. Torreses had been governing things there ever since, including his life.

"And that's why you came to Southwood?" Kenzie asked, suddenly feeling more than just a sexual connection to Ramon. For a moment she understood him. "To get away from your family?"

"When you say it like that, no, that's not the main reason, but a part of it," he explained. "I had everyone telling me what I needed to do with my life. And even if I started my life in Villa San Juan, I'd never truly know if I earned it or if I got it because of my name."

Under the glow of the passing streetlights, Kenzie nodded. "I get it. I felt the same way about winning Miss Southwood."

"But you won?"

"Narrowly," Kenzie said, nibbling her bottom lip and leaving out *no thanks to Erin*. Erin campaigned with and coached Kenzie's opponent.

"Well, there was more to me coming here than getting away from my folks," said Ramon. "I like helping out my cousins with the girls, Kimber and Philly."

"I never had Kimber in a tutoring session at Southwood High School," said Kenzie. "She always had her act together and never needed help."

"She is something else," Ramon agreed. "I don't know how many teenagers can lose both parents and manage to graduate as valedictorian."

"Don't forget, she's a Southern Style Glitz Queen," Kenzie said with a grin.

"Ah yes, the whole queen thing. It is beauty queen season around here."

Kenzie turned and smiled at him but as they drove by the old post office a light flashed on the first floor.

"What the hell?" Ramon maneuvered the truck to the curb and got out of the car without turning the engine off. A group of kids scattered from the front step and out from a broken window. There were too many of them to catch. Some even took sport in the game and ran parallel to each other, breezing right by Ramon, although he did reach for a few of them. By the time he returned to the car, Kenzie was in tears with laughter.

"I guess it's safe to say it's also teenager mischief season," Ramon grumbled, gripping the steering wheel.

Wiping the corners of her eyes, Kenzie said, "Now you see my reasoning for wanting some sort of youth center? These kids have nothing but idle time on their hands."

Ramon cast Kenzie a glance accompanied by a flat smirk.

"Too soon?" She asked him.

"Just wait until I get my second wind," Ramon growled before shaking his head and joining Kenzie's laughter with his own.

Chapter 5

"Everyone knows women are masterminds of revenge. The better the sex, the eviler their plans might be for you."

An echo of deep laughter from the other guests of Magnolia Palace filled the weight room the following morning. Nate Reyes and his wild comments were the exact reason Ramon made sure his hotel had two gyms. Ramon tried to finish his eighth rep of bench presses but his cousin's off-the-wall statement made it hard. Nate stood unapologetically by his statement with a straight face before he rubbed his hands together and reached for his dumbbells.

The three-hundred-and-seventy-five-pound weights clinked into place as Ramon struggled to catch his breath and he sat upright. The blurry vision of Stephen jumping rope became clearer. The comments didn't faze Stephen. Meanwhile the other men in the gym could no longer pretend to be into their own workouts. Everyone nodded as if agreeing with the statement. Southwood didn't have the *appropriate gym* Ramon needed to keep in shape so he'd made sure Magnolia Palace had one. His cousins made sure the facilities were constantly in use.

"Nate," Stephen scolded.

"Clearly, since Lexi is going to have your second child before your oldest is one——" Nate sighed, dragging his hand over his light brown face "——she hasn't worked out the kinks of you outbidding her on the piece of property she wanted to buy."

Ramon choked on his laughter.

"You're laughing but I don't know why, *primo*," Nate went on. "You volunteered to take a woman to two more weddings," Nate stated and added, "the same woman who had your car towed for being parked a fraction over the line near a fire hydrant by her fireman friend."

Ramon nodded his head and accepted the verbal taunts that were reminders of incidents between Kenzie and himself. At least now the antics would stop. If yesterday was an inkling of what a friendship between them would be like, Ramon couldn't wait to hang out with her again.

"Pay no attention to Nate," Stephen said with a chuckle. "He's still mad about fireman Parker Ward's history with Amelia."

"Hey, their history was in high school," Nate interrupted and puffed out his chest. "Amelia chose me."

By Ramon's calculations, Nate was the one who needed a history lesson. Before becoming Mrs. Reyes, Amelia had spent ten grand at a bachelor's auction just to get even with Nate. Of course, Ramon would love to hear what his cousin-in-law, the reality TV show producer, would do after hearing this non-scientific theory.

"Whatever, Nate," said Ramon. He reached down for his bottled water and took a long swig. The beverage cooled the heat in his chest. When he finished, he stood up to flex his muscles in the mirror. The black tank top he wore exposed the well-defined guns he took care of. Ramon lifted his arms, flexed and kissed his biceps.

"Primp all you want in the mirror," said Nate, "but you will never fetch ten Gs."

"Can we get back to this wedding business?" Stephen asked.

"What about it?" Ramon inquired.

"You don't have to make such a commitment just to secure your bid for the old post office," Stephen stated. *Always the voice of reason.* Ramon nodded his head and agreed with his older cousin. "There's always the archives section in the library."

Shaking his head, Nate cleared his throat. "Not really. I took Kimber last year for her final history project and she said she couldn't find anything good in there."

"I know," Ramon said with a shrug. "I prefer to study with a buddy."

Nate laughed in approval. "I ain't mad at you. I just want to make sure you're aware of the calculating ones."

"She's not a evil-genius-revenge-mastermind, Nate," Ramon verified.

"Does she show up at the same places you are?" asked one of the men at the pull-up bar.

"She's got this eagle eye," Nate answered. "She manages to know when he arrives someplace and finds a way to make his life miserable."

Nate's statement warranted a collective *hmph* from everyone.

"You're leaving out the main part, Nate. Amelia and Lexi have worked with Kenzie on numerous projects, so it's only natural we're at the same place at the same time."

Another round of disapproving *hmphs.*

I'm the one showing up places now, like the wedding last night."

"Wait, though—" Ramon struggled to gain control of the situation "—there is more to these weddings than

I thought. I can't let her face the wrath of her cousins. They're not like us."

Stephen sighed and laughed out loud. "Do you think Lourdes wants to face Rosa and her perfect husband at any wedding? Especially after being stood up at the altar?"

"That was cold." Ramon winced and recalled the time his then eighteen-year-old cousin Lourdes invited everyone down to Miami Beach for a wedding that never happened. At the last minute her fiancé chose business over love. Ramon inhaled deeply. He never wanted to be one to hurt his family but he understood the dude's perspective. Women wanted to be a certain weight before getting married. Why was it hard for women to understand men wanted to be financially ready?

"It's not like Lourdes is hurting in the financial department," said Nate. "I think she mentioned something about planning a wedding for one of the ex's brothers."

Last week Ramon had doubted Kenzie would lift a finger to help his family but after last night he was sure they'd made headway. Though she hadn't let him walk her to her apartment door, Kenzie had allowed him to drive her home. *It made sense to leave the wedding together*, she'd said.

What Kenzie had failed to say was the word *yes* to him. So should he attend the next wedding? According to Aunt Bren, a friend of the Hairstons was getting married and Kenzie was attending. A squeal from outside snapped Ramon out of his daydream.

"What is that noise?"

"Sounds like Jessilyn." Ramon chuckled. "My new chef gets excited when the food she ordered arrives on time."

Stephen rubbed his stomach. "My kind of cook."

"Are y'all staying for lunch? The guests this week are from Canada, so Jessi thought it would be a treat for them to try some down-home cooking." Ramon made sure to use the Southern drawl he'd perfected over the past few months. "I'm sure she'd be happy to fix extra."

"I'm sure she won't mind." Nate patted his stomach.

"I'll take anyone's cooking over his," said Stephen, hiking his thumb toward his brother.

"Hey."

Ramon shook his head and laughed. "Great. I'll let her know to set a few more plates."

Exiting the gym, Ramon thought about his cousin's words. Nate was a hoot and would deny everything if Amelia heard him talk. No... Kenzie disproved Nate's theory. She was sane and damn near gifted in bed. Ramon's body stiffened at the memory of her beneath and on top of him.

Before stopping by the kitchen to give the lunch order, Ramon headed toward his office on the first floor to grab his phone before taking a shower. He took in a deep breath at the banister in his sprawling digs and shook his head. This was his. There were times he still couldn't believe he turned a dilapidated plantation home into a thriving hotel. All sixteen rooms were booked for the entire summer. Guests buzzed through the foyer, prepared to get out on the lake. Children waddled barefoot with brightly colored pool-floaties around their arms and bellies. A lifeguard was already on duty, had been since sunup, for the sake of the guests who wanted an early-morning row out on the calm water.

Ramon slipped into his study to glance at his schedule. He'd learned from Kenzie to write things down on a planner instead of just assuming he'd remember things. Thank God for her. Kenzie had her act together, whereas the ladies he dated in the past were a bit on the vapid side, concerning themselves with climbing the social ladder. He smiled to himself and breezed over to his desk. The blotter listed off all the activities scheduled for the guests. For himself, he had nothing on the schedule. With the help of his chef and housekeeping staff, this place ran itself. Ramon coordinated the activities by a signup sheet when the guests registered. Maybe he'd travel into town today and accidentally run into Kenzie. It was odd his heart skipped a beat at the thought of her name.

Anxiety over how she might seek revenge against him always lingered in the back of his mind. Could Nate's words be true? Was she a vengeful mastermind tricking him to fall for her, just to reject him down the line? Nah, he laughed off the idea. But today's nerves were more from excitement. He learned last night Kenzie didn't want to tie him down. *Not like tying up is off the bedroom menu*, he thought with a devilish grin.

Satisfied with his free schedule, Ramon headed out of his office down the hall toward the oversize kitchen in the back. He spotted Jessilyn seated at the table with an abnormally large bowl piled high with fresh green beans.

"There's the man of the hour." Jessilyn beamed. "We were just talking about you."

A few weeks ago Jessilyn had approached Ramon about a job opportunity. She was young, fresh out of culinary school and needed a chance. He tested her with a few of his grandmother's recipes, tasted her specialties and agreed to give her a chance this summer.

"We?" Ramon asked.

When he stepped farther into the kitchen he spotted the backside of another person seated adjacent to Jessilyn. Red hair piled on top of her head and twisted into a tight bun, Kenzie turned in her chair to face him. He swore her fresh, freckled face lit up at the sight of him.

"We were," Kenzie answered. She stood up and smoothed

down her turquoise sundress. Freckles were sprinkled across her shoulders. He remembered kissing them last summer.

Ramon gulped. "Hey, I was hoping I'd run into you today."

Kenzie's left brow rose. "Afraid I'd run off with your jacket?"

"Huh?"

Reaching onto the chair next to her Kenzie lifted the jacket he'd wrapped around her last night when they stepped out of the church. "I forgot to give this back to you when you dropped me off."

"Oh?" Jessilyn breathed, giving life to a potential rumor.

"It wasn't like that," Kenzie said, shooting down the gossip. "Ramon helped me out of a sticky situation at Corie's wedding."

"How'd that go?"

"It was lovely."

"So were her groomsmen," Jessilyn said with a giggle. "They were out partying up at the club in Samaritan."

The only nightclub Ramon had gone to was Throb. It didn't surprise him to hear the basketball players were hanging out there. Anything trendy came through Samaritan. Southwood preserved the important history of the area. Ramon had partied a few times at Club Throb. Peachville, well, the name spoke for itself. This season Ramon made sure every room in the hotel had a bowl of fresh peaches.

"Hence why you were out of it when I saw you this morning," Kenzie said to Jessilyn.

Ramon lifted his brows and Jessilyn hit Kenzie playfully in the shoulder and shushed her. While Ramon enjoyed his chef's cooking, he understood she was young and made some irresponsible decisions, such as going out when she had work in the morning. As long as she came to the kitchen ready to work, he wasn't going to judge.

"Do I need to be concerned?" Ramon asked.

"Not at all," said Jessilyn. "Kenzie was just helping me finish up snapping the beans and then I'll start lunch."

"Great, that's why I came to see you," said Ramon. "I have my cousins downstairs working out and they want to stay for lunch."

The idea of cooking for more people didn't faze Jessilyn one bit. As a matter of fact her smile broadened. "I'll make sure they have plenty."

"They have wives," reminded Kenzie as she returned the playful swat against Jessilyn's forearm.

"Sheesh."

Ramon pressed his lips together for a moment. Kenzie, however, did not bother trying to contain herself. Her infectious laugh brought all of them to a full chuckle.

"Seriously, though." Jessilyn sobered. "Bring whomever you wish. Kenzie really saved the day snapping these beans with me."

"Kenzie—" Ramon cleared his throat "—would you like to stay for lunch?"

"Thanks but," she began, rising from her seat, "I have plans."

With whom? Ramon's mind screamed and then he glanced down at the ground and wondered if the hem of her dress covered her purple-polished toes he'd spied last night. "We have mimosas if you're interested."

"Thanks, but I better get going. I really stopped by to return your jacket."

Without thinking, the two of them began walking out of the kitchen. "I could have picked up the jacket next week when we attend Felicia's wedding."

"I'm supposed to meet up with some friends at Felicia's wedding," said Kenzie. "I don't know if I'll be there or stay late to catch up with them."

Ramon clasped his hands behind his back. "But we're still going?"

"I haven't agreed to your proposal."

Shaking his head, Ramon kept walking. Their footsteps were drowned out by the children screaming with excitement. He liked the way Kenzie smiled at them. "Let me guess, you've got canoeing on the agenda."

"I do. How'd you guess?"

"Been there, done that," Kenzie said, looking up and batting her lashes. "Or have you forgotten?"

"How could anyone forget how this home once belonged to the famous Swaynes of Southwood, who so graciously opened the doors for public access for vacations?" Ramon imitated Kenzie's Southern drawl as he spoke. When he bowed at the waist Kenzie pushed her hand against his shoulder.

"Don't get hurt," teased Kenzie.

"Sorry, I couldn't help myself." Ramon grabbed hold of Kenzie's hand before she poked him for a second time. Kenzie wiggled her fingers against his. Everything else in the room ceased for him. The noise of the children, the dishes clanking in the dining room and the screeches from the teenagers outside went away. He was sweaty from his workout but touching Kenzie brought a whole new level of heat.

"Did you really come here to return my jacket?"

"I did," said Kenzie. She stopped struggling against his grip. "And I wanted to thank you for showing up last night like you did."

Ramon jutted his chin outward. "I was pretty heroic."

"Dear Lord," Kenzie groaned.

"What? I came in looking all sharp and won your family over."

Kenzie rolled her eyes and blew a lock of her red hair out of her face. "First of all, Erin is nosey and hung on to your every word to get the tea."

"And Auntie Bren?" Ramon genuinely liked the matriarch of the Hairston side of the family. Like Kenzie, Auntie Bren was tightly wound with a pile of red hair on top of her head, although Ramon suspected a hairdresser might be helping her by now. Either way, both women were firecrackers.

"Don't call her that," Kenzie said from between gritted teeth.

"She asked me to." Ramon gave Kenzie's fingers a squeeze. "Are you jealous?"

"Of?"

"Of the idea of Auntie Bren wanting me."

"I'm leaving now." Kenzie yawned. She yanked her hand free once more and freed herself.

Ramon stopped himself from taking a step forward and capturing her in his arms. "Hot date?" Too bad he couldn't stop his mouth from saying anything stupid.

The corners of Kenzie's mouth turned up into a grin. "Didn't you have your own date Friday night?"

"If by date you mean a slumber party here at Magnolia Palace for my preteen niece after taking her and her friends to a concert in the park down from your apartment. Maybe you heard it?"

Judging from the look on her face, Ramon guessed she had. Also accompanying the annoyed look was a flash of relief. Was she happy to know he hadn't been on a date?

"How sweet of you," Kenzie finally said.

"Sweet was letting those girls do my hair."

Kenzie covered her face to hide her laugh. Her eyes

crinkled at the corners and gave her attempt away. "Please tell me there are pictures."

"None I'm willing to share. Besides, you might try to blackmail me into escorting you to your events."

"Really?" Kenzie cocked her hand on her hip and rolled her eyes.

"Nah, I'm still waiting on you to say yes to my offer," said Ramon. "Remember, I still need you to teach me about the history of the post office so I can decide what to propose for the planning committee." Reaching for the door, Ramon held on to the jamb. Kenzie paused under his arm. Sun backlit her face like a halo. "I need your help, Kenzie."

Wordlessly Kenzie ducked under his arm. Like a puppy he followed her to a white convertible with pink leather seats. They both reached for her door at the same time. Electricity bolted through his skin.

Kenzie had to have felt it, too. She rubbed her hand. A red tint spread over her freckled cheeks. Kenzie cleared her throat. "Well, I am off this month but I've got a few new items to archive, so my desk isn't overflowing when I get back."

"What do you do there?" he asked.

"Well," she started, "I am a historian for the town but that's all glorified. Basically I am a city worker. Until I have my own space, I am an archivist, as in, I'm bringing Southwood's history into the digital age."

She certainly knew a lot about the town, he thought to himself.

"Meet me in my office at City Hall tomorrow," she said. "We can talk there."

Ramon nodded and waited before Kenzie got in her car and headed down the drive before turning toward the wide porch. Nate and Stephen waited for him.

"So she just happened to be here at Magnolia Palace?" Nate asked.

"Shut up, Nate," Ramon said with a laugh as he flipped his cousin the middle finger.

"Well, I hadn't heard from you so I thought I'd check and see if you ended up eloping with Mr. Save-the-Day," Maggie's voice sang out from the cell phone on the corner of Kenzie's desk.

Though they weren't on video chat, Kenzie rolled her eyes toward the florescent lights of her office. "Please don't ruin my Monday with any of your craziness," said Kenzie.

So far Kenzie's month off work wasn't turning out as she'd planned. Monday morning, knowing Alexander intended to sell off—on behalf of the city—all the property downtown, Kenzie came in to work to check and secure all requests. Her morning started out with a tutoring session with one of the football players from Southwood High as a favor to the parents. After the first session ended quickly, the potential quarterback came in for tutoring and thirty minutes stretched into close to lunchtime, as her second appointment took longer than she anticipated.

A stack of requests from local businesses for historic preservation teetered on her desk. Everyone coveted a prestigious plaque posted on their buildings. It helped garner more tourists. This was the part of her job she loved. She followed the paper trail to verify each claim. Even though she grew up in Southwood, she loved hearing the stories people passed on from generation to generation. The only thing she hated about her job was having to tell people no. The last time Kenzie denied a family entry into the registry she felt horrible, but in retrospect, having a peach in the shape of Fat Albert did not make the home or land historic. Ever since Kenzie took on the job as town historian last year she had been busy.

"Don't act like you can't hear me," Maggie persisted. "You're not even supposed to be working. Don't tell me Alexander made you come in."

"Alexander can't make me do anything," Kenzie said with a frown. Thank God Margaret gave her his summer schedule. It was bad enough she was going to have to see him this weekend for Felicia's wedding. How many folks in his family were going to recommend they give each other another shot? Kenzie would rather eat a bowl of rocks. "He never comes in Mondays."

"So why are you there when you're off?"

"I helped out the Stanfield boy about a half an hour ago and then I noticed some work that must have come in when I left early Friday. I wanted to take a peek at some of the homes and businesses requesting to be on the docket for preservation this fall."

"So?"

"So I can take a look at these places this month and maybe even have an announcement for the entries to the state historic registry at the sesquicentennial."

"For which you'll have a date, right? Auntie Bren told me Danielle and Michelle were proposed to last night."

Of course her other Hairston cousins would follow suit and get married. Dani was a physical therapist and Michelle worked with Erin in Orlando, Florida, at their big-time sports agency. "You should have seen their rings. Auntie Bren was going on about the rocks."

"For crying out loud," Kenzie moaned. "I have a freaking PhD."

"So?"

"So?" Kenzie snorted. "Paper beats rock every single time."

Maggie's sigh caused a static sound through the phone. "You say that now, but wait until you have your own set of gems."

"I have my own," she responded, "It's called the Miss Southwood crown. Since I won—"

"Oh-so long ago," Maggie interjected.

"No one on either side of the Hairston and Swayne family has won since."

"Whatever. What's going on with you and Ramon? Is he escorting you to Felicia's wedding?"

A smile tugged at the corners of Kenzie's mouth. Heat spread across her cheeks at the memory of Ramon asking her the same thing. "I haven't really accepted his offer."

"I thought I heard you say you would help."

"I'm helping anyone who wants to place a bid on the historic buildings in Southwood, not just Ramon. There are other places up to be sold. And as the town's historian…"

Maggie grumbled on the other end of the line. "You're the only person with the credentials who can help."

"The only way I can help is to make sure the buyers are aware of the historicity of the structure," Kenzie said, trying to sound authoritative. "Whoever buys one of the buildings downtown has to keep in mind they can't just add a porch to accommodate, let's say, a sports bar. They'll have to stick with the original work as close as possible on the interior and exterior."

"Let me guess, you're going to give an extra lesson to the person who is going to put in a business of your choice, right?"

"Dear older and much wiser sister," Kenzie said, "you know me so well."

"What I do know is you and Ramon were a hit at Corie's wedding. Auntie Bren is looking forward to dancing with him at Felicia's wedding—she said something about making some man jealous."

The last thing Kenzie wanted to do was encourage Auntie Bren to get close to Ramon. What would it look like for two grown men to be fighting over an old lady? Besides, Kenzie didn't want to get comfortable with the idea of Ramon taking her anywhere. What if he decided to stop helping and stood her up for one of the events? It happened before. Kenzie hated being humiliated and the memory of waiting for Ramon to pick her up for the final crowning for last year's Miss Southwood Beauty Pageant was still fresh. The two of them had spent the entire week together; it had been only natural for everyone to assume they'd arrive together. She'd spent that whole evening avoiding questions about his whereabouts and the pitying glances from the people involved with the pageant. Being embarrassed was one thing but she couldn't take being the subject of a year's worth of gossip. Not again.

"Everyone has been talking about you two… Speaking of which, why didn't you come to church yesterday?"

Kenzie choked on the air. Her eyes watered. "What? You went to church?"

"I had to get my church on. I'm not a complete heathen."

"Of course not."

The elevators outside her door dinged and Kenzie's heart raced with the idea of Ramon coming to visit her here. This was her playing field. He couldn't charm her or throw her off her game. Here she was a professional.

"Damn," some of the ladies by the water cooler collectively sang out.

The sweet smell of magnolias filled the air. The pit of her stomach dropped and her nipples became acutely aware of his presence. *He was here.*

A bouquet of blooming magnolias filled the doorway

and covered his face. Kenzie found herself leaning in her black leather chair for a glimpse. He wore a pair of khaki pants with a blue sports coat. His massive hands wrapped around a thin paper blanket cradling the bouquet.

"Ramon," Kenzie breathed. She stood up from her chair and the back of it hit the wall.

"Ramon's there?" Maggie's voice came from the pink cell phone.

As Kenzie maneuvered around her desk, she swiped the screen to disconnect the call and pulled down her black pencil skirt. The peach silk blouse she wore clung to the skin on her back.

"Hi," Kenzie said, trying to play it cool. She clasped her hands behind her back.

Ramon lowered the flowers to reveal his devastatingly handsome smile. "Aren't you going to take these?"

"Well, I wasn't sure. The last time you arrived at my doorstep with flowers you made sure to let me know they were for another woman."

"A preteen niece," said Ramon, pushing the flowers toward her. "And I thought I explained about the concert."

If ever there was a time to crawl into a hole, it was now. How jealous did she sound? "Well, thank you then." She accepted the flowers and glanced around for a vase. "I'm afraid I don't have anything here to put these in."

"We can head back to your place."

Kenzie offered him a tight smile. "No thanks."

"How about lunch?" Ramon asked. "Have you eaten yet?"

"One of my students brought me a muffin earlier."

Ramon leaned against the door. She hated to admit how cramped he appeared in her office. "A muffin, huh? Sounds like a great, healthy choice."

"You know once you lick the frosting off a cupcake it

becomes a muffin, so that counts, right?" she joked and rolled her eyes when he smirked. Kenzie pressed her lips together. "Whatever, we can do lunch. It's not Food Truck Thursday, but there are a few locals, and we can meet up with everyone."

"Everyone?"

There was no mistaking the disappointment in his voice. He didn't bother covering his feelings with a tawdry grin. Kenzie inhaled deeply and steadied her libido. "Yes. I mentioned before you're not the only one interested in property around town. So since Alexander is serious about selling off vacant pieces, to generate revenue for the town, I thought I'd give everyone a history lesson."

Ramon's upper lip curled. "Uh, didn't you already tutor today?"

"What are you here for?" Kenzie turned with her butt against her desk. Ramon cocked his head to the side and licked his lips. A team of goose bumps marched along her arms. All he needed to do was kick the door closed and in two seconds flat she'd be his.

"I thought you were going to give me a private lesson about Southwood," he said, advancing closer.

"You thought we'd do it alone?"

Thankfully someone behind them cleared their throat in a soft manner.

"Kenzie," said Margaret as she cleared her throat at the doorway. "The *package* I thought shipped out is on its way back here."

Alexander. Kenzie sighed to prevent her upper lip from curling. "Thanks, Miss Margaret," she said sweetly. "By the way, this is Ramon Torres. Ramon, this is Miss Margaret Foley."

Charming as ever, Ramon kissed the back of Margaret's hand. "Pleasure to meet you."

Margaret, fifty years of age, beamed. For the last six months Margaret had decided she was going to stop coloring her hair and embrace the gray. Right now a trim of gray circled her head like a headband. She blushed and batted her eyelashes in Kenzie's direction. "Well, hello."

"Foley, you say?" Ramon cut his eyes at Kenzie. Her heart thumped against her rib cage. "One of the footlockers in the basement of the post office belonged to a Priscilla Foley. Any relation?"

After a moment of thinking and twisting her lips, Margaret shook her head. "Not that I can think. I'll let you know if I can remember anyone by that name. Okay?"

"Don't worry about it," Kenzie replied, remembering why Alexander's secretary was here in the first place. "We were heading out for lunch. Can we bring you anything back?"

"Aren't you sweet? But you're supposed to be off work for the rest of this month, dear."

"Yes, ma'am." Kenzie did not miss the way Ramon cocked his eyebrow toward her. The last thing she wanted was him aware of her free time.

"Good. Now, you two go on and grab some lunch." From the door, Margaret shooed the two of them out of Kenzie's cramped office and picked up the flowers. "I'll get these sent over to your apartment, okay, Kenzie? I also got a call from the front desk—the other person interested in the old post office is waiting downstairs for you."

Kenzie reached around and grabbed the stack of requests and her purse off the coat rack beside the door. "All right. I'll get in touch with these people."

"Mr. Torres." Margaret drew her attention to the man taking the folders from Kenzie's hands. "I expect you to make sure Kenzie has a good time."

"Oh yes, ma'am."

One of the ladies from the office already pressed the button for them and Ramon and Kenzie entered wordlessly. Once the door closed, Ramon shifted the paperwork under his arm and leaned against the wall. "Did we just get kicked out of your office?"

If that's what Ramon needed to believe, then sure. Kenzie did not want to bring up her past relationship or scarred friendship with Alexander. And she definitely did not want Alexander to try to sell Ramon another building.

"Margaret is sweet."

"And so you're off for the month?" Ramon asked.

The light in the elevator lit up and dinged with each floor. Kenzie concentrated on the numbers. "Yep."

"Great," Ramon exclaimed. "How about I take off and you can deal with the person who is going to lose the bid to me?"

Kenzie laughed. "Confident, aren't you?"

"Always."

"What if this person listens to my suggestion for what to do with the place?"

Ramon waved off the notion with his free hand. "I've got this. Southwood needs a martial arts or CrossFit gym and I am sure everyone on this council panel is going to agree with me."

"A gym?" Kenzie balked and frowned. She could imagine oversize, bulky men in tank tops and women dressed in see-through yoga pants walking through the center to get to the establishment. "Please don't."

"All right." Ramon laughed out loud. "That was me just being vindictive against one of my cousins. What about a smoothie shop?"

The light lit up on three. Was the elevator slower than before?

"Okay, I get it. Dry cleaner?"

Kenzie rolled her eyes. "Southwood has one in the Brickler Hotel off Main Street."

"You want me to walk my clothes into enemy territory?"

"You're worried about Brickler Hotel when the Brutti Hotel sits smack-dab in the middle of Four Points Park?"

"They're a chain," said Ramon. "It's not the same or as historic as the original structure of the first hotel in Southwood."

The history fact won him brownie points. "You're the one who decided to turn Magnolia Palace into a hotel," Kenzie reminded him with a wink.

Winking in his direction didn't help her at all. Ramon flashed a smile and Kenzie prayed for the elevator to stop midfloor. Caving in to Ramon's decadent lips would be justified if the circumstances deemed it so. Unfortunately the elevator kept going. In anticipation of reaching the ground floor Kenzie reached for her paperwork. Ramon held on to it, managing to tug her close to him.

"Why are you doing this?" Kenzie asked.

"What?" He had the nerve to sound innocent. "I'm trying to be chivalrous. Haven't we moved beyond the hostility between us?"

"There's nothing between us," Kenzie lied.

The smirk on his face proved he didn't believe her, either. "We need to get some things out of the way before we work together on this post office proposal and Felicia's wedding. All this tension between us is going to make Auntie Bren wonder."

"Stop calling her that," Kenzie started to squawk. Before she knew it, Ramon had lowered his hand and captured her lips with his.

Any sense of irritation or anger fell to the wayside. Kenzie pressed her hands against Ramon's broad chest. Her thumbs brushed against the buttons of his oxford shirt, tempting her to rip the material open. The familiar dance of their tongues excited her. Ramon broke the kiss and straightened to his full height. Kenzie wanted to smack and kiss him at the same time.

"Good," he breathed, "I needed to get that out of the way."

Maybe they *had* needed to kiss—to get these confusing feelings out of their system. The problem? She wanted more.

The doors opened. Guiltily, Kenzie took a large step backward.

"Hey, just the person I'm looking for," Erin said cheerfully. She stepped inside and wrapped her arms around Kenzie's shoulders. "I hear you're the one who's going to show me the old post office."

Chapter 6

The heavy knock on the apartment door the following Saturday morning led Kenzie to believe Maggie had not yet arrived. Someone masculine stood on the other side and Kenzie assumed it would be her brother, Richard, who, like the rest of her family members, had come into town. Wrapping her pink terry cloth robe tighter around her waist, Kenzie yanked the door open. Instead of the reddish-haired brother she expected to see, Kenzie came face-to-face with Ramon Torres. Thanks to attending practice with her niece Bailey for moral support for the pageant, Kenzie hadn't run into Ramon for the rest of the week. She thought Ramon might have been scared off listening to the bickering between her and Erin. She shot down Erin's idea for building a rehab clinic for athletes in Southwood. Erin felt downtown Southwood was perfect for rehabilitating patients. Kenzie found her cousin ridiculous. Sports figures would only bring in reporters and disturb the quiet. At one point Kenzie hushed Ramon for defending Erin and because of it, she was sure Ramon was intentionally avoiding her. But just because she didn't see him during the day didn't mean he wasn't haunting her dreams.

How many nights had she woken up from fevered dreams since the kiss back at City Hall? The night after the post office tour Kenzie had dreamed of what would have happened in the elevator. What was it with them and elevators? Finding him now standing in front of her gave Kenzie pause and she wondered if she'd fallen asleep after her shower this afternoon. She blinked her eyes and he didn't disappear.

"I truly need to start asking who it is," Kenzie said with her hand still on the door.

Ramon's dark eyes glanced over her body. "Or you could look through the peeph—" He cut his words off by covering his mouth with his large hands, stifling a laugh. His dark eyes roamed her body, then his head cocked to the side. When their eyes met, he dropped his hand and chuckled. "Sorry, I wasn't going for the short jokes."

"Whatever." Kenzie offered him a dramatic eye roll and straightened to her five-foot-three height. She'd known him for almost a year, slept with him after a week of knowing him, and yet this was the second time Ramon had appeared at her door. The one time she'd expected him to show up for her, he hadn't. Kenzie gripped the handle until her knuckles felt tight, but she remembered they'd called a truce to their feud. Unfortunately she couldn't stop the tone of annoyance in her voice. "Why are you here?"

Ramon didn't bother waiting for Kenzie to invite him; he simply strolled into her living room, wearing an inky black suit with a white-and-cerulean-striped oxford and a matching cerulean blue print tie. Kenzie blinked several times and glanced toward her bedroom where her dress hung on a soft padded hanger on the door. Lexi had designed the dress just for her.

The bedroom. Kenzie's heart skipped a beat. Ramon was here...in her place, with only a robe covering her body.

If he attempted to reach under the fabric, she doubted she'd want to stop him. *Damn his kisses*, she swore to herself and followed Ramon into her living room. He stood in front of the mantel of her fireplace where her framed PhD rested next to her Miss Southwood tiara.

"Felicia's wedding starts in an hour," he said out loud with his back to her.

After an appreciative stare at his backside, Kenzie said a silent prayer for strength to keep from giving into the idea of tempting this man for a romp on her couch. But if she did…thank God she'd cleaned up this morning. It wasn't like she had anything else to do this morning. In order to avoid Ramon or anyone else in her family, Kenzie had hid out in her apartment and ordered takeout for the week. With not having to step outside Kenzie figured she could remain in here for the remainder of her month-long vacation. If she decided to show up at Felicia's wedding, she could do so at the last minute and leave the first chance she got.

"Still doesn't explain why you stopped by." Kenzie sidled up next to her houseguest. "I never agreed to your proposal."

"I know," Ramon said, glancing down. "This isn't part of the proposal. As sweet as she is, I'm scared to death of Auntie Bren."

"Stop calling her that."

He didn't and continued annoying her. "Auntie Bren and I ran into each other at The Cupcakery and we shared a table together. She mentioned how good it was seeing you so happy last weekend and mumbled something about you dating a murderer. Perhaps I heard wrong."

"Great," Kenzie groaned and made eye contact with Ramon. "You heard Auntie Bren correctly," she clarified. "And I'm not dating a murderer."

"That's a relief." Ramon sighed.

"That I'm not dating a murderer or not dating period?"

Ramon's deep laugh echoed against her cream-colored walls. "Both."

"You didn't think I would be dating anyone?" Kenzie's hands moved to her hips.

"Need I remind you of your predicament for the month?" Ramon reached for her hands. The pads of his fingers stroked the length of her thumbs. The intimate touch sent a shiver down her spine. "If you were dating someone, he'd be a fool to not be here for you."

Kenzie's lips formed an O. Why, whenever he was this close, did he make her feel like a stereotypical lovesick fool? Her knees threatened to buckle and her lips threatened to twitch into a pucker and her heartbeat sped up. Ramon dipped his head low and cocked it to the side until their mouths neared. His thick lashes blinked as he looked down at her lips. Kenzie's throat went dry. She inhaled deeply and exhaled and tried to ignore the fact that she was naked as a jaybird beneath the robe. The faint smell of his fresh and woodsy cologne filled the tight space of air between them. The scent was just enough to set her nostrils open. *Wide-open*, as Auntie Bren would say, whenever a person was aroused. Kenzie exhaled a shaky breath and took a step backward.

"Auntie Bren expects to see us together tonight." Ramon smirked, straightened and turned back to the mantel. He adjusted a skewed photograph on the wall of Kenzie and her family at one of Maggie's charity Southwood events she hosted where everyone got together, including Richard. Despite the genuine smile on Richard's face that evening, her brother hated the limelight. Maggie and Kenzie often thought their parents must have found him on the stoop as a baby.

Ramon's hands swiped across the glass protecting her doctorate. A vulnerable shiver ran across her skin. "Why isn't this hanging in your office?"

Kenzie rolled her eyes. "Have you seen the size of my office?"

"Yes?"

"This thing will take over the space," she explained. "Besides, I don't need a document to tell everyone who I am or what my job is."

Ramon nodded and smiled for a moment, as if contemplating what she'd said. "You're right. Everyone does know who you are."

Was he teasing her again? Kenzie crossed her arms against under her breasts and raised a brow. "Meaning?"

"Meaning the Swaynes are an important part of the making of Southwood."

It was hard not to grin at a time like this. Kenzie realized Ramon had been paying attention during the tour she gave downtown earlier this week. Erin, with her ridiculous idea of moving back to Southwood, had failed to remember the Hairstons' contribution to the town history. She kept trying to interject her knowledge. Barry Hairston, Erin's great-great-great-grandfather, had been a founder, but he'd been a farmer and hadn't built anything in town. It was important to Kenzie that anyone buying downtown property respected the painstaking work her ancestors had done when they built this town. She wanted to remind them of what it took for African-American families to prosper post–Civil War. Reconstruction was a hard time for families starting over. In Southwood, the town came together to educate and protect one another.

"Do I get an A for remembering?"

"I am not a teacher," Kenzie replied.

Ramon scratched the back of his head. He wore his hair

in a bun on top of his head, which shook with the motion of his long fingers. Kenzie licked her lips. "Pardon me, but weren't you tutoring some kids Monday?"

"Tutoring and substitute teaching is more like it," said Kenzie.

"Your degree is in history, *Dr.* Swayne," he said.

A twinge jolted her heart. "No one ever calls me that."

"You earned it. Maybe I'll start calling you Dr. Swayne regularly." Ramon wiggled his brows up and down. "Or do you prefer to be called Miss Southwood?" He brushed the back of his hand across the crystals of the three-foot-high crown propped up on a small table by the shelf.

"I'm proud of both titles," said Kenzie. She squared her shoulders.

"Is it because you're the last Swayne queen?"

Kenzie bit the inside of her cheeks to prevent from laughing. "Erin meant to embarrass me with that the other night."

"Why?" Ramon asked as he turned toward her with a raised brow.

"Because she knows I don't like to be embarrassed," Kenzie said with a shrug. "Cousin rivalry, I guess."

"Maybe cousin adoration?" Ramon suggested. "I don't know how many cousins consider moving to a town to be with family they dislike."

No, Kenzie thought to herself. Ramon and his cousins were close. She refused to believe Erin seriously wanted to move back to Southwood to open a clinic for pampered athletes. Kenzie decided she needed to confront Erin this evening. But she didn't want Ramon around for it.

"You don't have to take me to the wedding."

"Of course I do," Ramon said. "I got all decked out in this coordinating suit, just as Lexi suggested."

"You did what?"

"Lexi is my family," he replied. "You don't think I wouldn't call and confirm what she made for you?"

Kenzie pressed her hand to her heart. "Seriously?"

"Yes."

Ramon sighed and clasped his hands behind his back. Kenzie's heart beat faster with his nearness. Without even touching her he made her body shiver. "Now, if you'd rather stay here and continue our kisses…" Kenzie backed up until her legs pressed against the back of the love seat. He closed the gap between them and pressed his hand to the back of her neck. The touch sent a spark through her.

Kenzie's eyes rolled back with her deep sigh, as she hoped to blow out the tension building in her blood. "Last week was because Auntie Bren was watching and I thought the kiss in the elevator was to get this tension out of our systems." Kenzie didn't realize her voice was barely above a whisper until Ramon leaned close. She thought for a moment he couldn't hear but instead, his breath tickled her right earlobe.

"You will never be out of my system."

Kenzie gulped. She clutched closed the opening of her robe. Ramon covered her hand with his and eased her fingers free from the material. The warmth of his hand cupped her breast. Kenzie took a deep intake of breath before biting her bottom lip. She tilted her head backward as Ramon nibbled her neck and then collarbone in that exact spot that sexually charged her body.

Every spot of her body he touched set her skin on fire. While his mouth made its way down her breastbone, Ramon slid his large hand through the opening of the robe. His fingers splayed against the curve of her stomach. While his thumb traced a circle around her navel, four fingers dipped into the curls between her legs. Kenzie sucked in a sharp breath. Pleasure oozed through her pores.

To fix the height difference between them, Ramon lifted Kenzie onto the back of her sofa. Legs dangling, Kenzie clung to Ramon's shoulders and arched her back to meet his mouth for a deep kiss. He felt wonderful. She felt free. No worries in the world. This is what she remembered about Ramon and oh God, how she'd missed this. Ramon's hands moved from around her waist back to the valley between her legs. He kissed her lips and played with her clitoris, rolling it between his thumb and forefinger. His middle finger slid inside of her body. Ramon knew her. He knew when to deepen his kiss and the pressure of his finger. He knew how to bring her right to the brink of an orgasm and when to break the kiss, take both breasts in his hands and suck on her nipples at the same time. Kenzie floated on air. She fell backward on the chair but Ramon caught her before she flipped over. A forefinger stroked the length of her neck as it extended back.

"What's it going to be, Dr. Beauty Queen?" Ramon whispered. He helped her to her feet and readjusted the ties of her robe.

"I think we better leave before my alleged murderer date finds himself free tonight." Kenzie smiled to herself as she headed toward her bedroom and left Ramon in her living room with his eyes open wide.

The Presbyterian church off the corner of Main Street was once again packed later that afternoon. Most of the shops in town closed early on Saturdays, which made getting to the church and parking easy. Ramon and Kenzie arrived just before the ceremony started. They found seats in the back rows. It was easy to spot the Hairstons among the guests in attendance. Auntie Bren had craned her neck to find them. When he waved in her direction, Auntie Bren smiled in approval. Ramon didn't miss Kenzie's elbow in his ribs. The bride was beautiful—well, Ramon had a hard time trying to concentrate on anything else besides his date. He deserved a medal of honor for controlling himself in Kenzie's apartment. How the hell was he going to spend the rest of the evening next to her keeping his hands to himself? The woman was sexy in clothes and out. The low-cut blue dress she wore was not helping Ramon keep his head. A row of pretty flowers lined the bodice of the gown and kept beckoning his eyes. The nuptials for her friend, Felicia, didn't take long and Kenzie shot out of her seat once the service ended.

The Ward-Crawford reception was held at the new hotel overlooking Four Points Park, convenient for the other three surrounding cities. Gianni Brutti, the owner of the hotel, sent over a limousine service for the wedding party, even though the weather was perfect for everyone to walk. Kenzie insisted they drive so she didn't have to run into anyone she knew. Was she embarrassed by him? A cloud of childhood shame briefly washed over him as he remembered the lonely feeling when no one wanted to pick him to be on their sports teams. Ramon might have been a heavy child but he would have been a heavy hitter too, if the kids had given him the chance. It felt like everyone was embarrassed by him.

Because they had left the church earlier than the others to avoid talking to everyone, Ramon and Kenzie arrived at the reception early. They were able to grab a drink at the bar before entering the gold-and-glass elevators to the party.

"I can't believe I am standing here," Kenzie groaned.

Had Gianni not been a close friend of the Torres family, Ramon might have grumbled the same way as Kenzie, but for a different reason. He should feel threatened by Gianni's fifteen-story hotel. Gianni had capitalized on the location of the building and garnered visitors who wanted a closer to town southern visit with all the city life amenities—an upscale restaurant and bar inside, close to the woods without being in nature.

"You don't like one of the nation's best hotels?" Ramon asked.

"Need I remind you this place is your competition?" said Kenzie.

Ramon pressed his hand against Kenzie's lower back to help her sit down on the bar stool. "I didn't realize you cared so much about my business," he said, his mouth close to her earlobe.

Kenzie turned her face toward him. Their mouths were close. A set of goose bumps christened Kenzie's shoulders. "I care," she whispered, tilting her head. Ramon's heart raced, eager for a continuation of their last encounter. "You're living in my ancestral home."

"Cute," said Ramon. He touched the tip of her nose with his index finger and signaled the bartender for two glasses of champagne.

"Are we celebrating something?" Kenzie asked.

"Yes," Ramon replied, taking both glasses from the bartender. "After a day like today, shouldn't we?" A red blush stained Kenzie's cheeks. He liked that about her. For all her toughness, Kenzie had a vulnerable side.

"Ramon," Kenzie began as she cleared her throat, "about this afternoon… Don't you think things got a little out of hand?"

"Not a damn bit," he swore. "We are good together, Kenzie. Don't you agree?"

Kenzie tried to hide her smile by taking a sip of her champagne. He knew she agreed. He didn't need to hear her verbally agree.

"There's more to a relationship than sex."

"So there was more to the relationship between you and this previous guy you dated?" asked Ramon.

"Alleged." Kenzie smiled coyly and wiggled her brows.

A cackle of women's laughter sounded off from the entrance of the hotel's bar. The two of them turned around in their seats. A group Ramon recognized as part of the wedding party and some guests filled the doorway. Each woman wore at least a five-inch tiara on top of her head and screamed at the sight of Kenzie, who slipped off her chair and met the girls in the center of the bar. They all began to jump up and down, screaming with excitement. The group turned in one huge circle and he suddenly noticed a sparkling tiara nestled in Kenzie's curly hair. Ramon blinked twice. When did she get a tiara? She hadn't left the house with it, right? They'd sat through the wedding and Ramon was pretty sure she hadn't been wearing it.

Once the screams died down, Kenzie joined Ramon's side and slipped her hand into the crook of his arm. "Ramon," she said with sweetness in her voice and a squeeze of her hand on his biceps. He wasn't going to question it.

"Yes, dear?"

"These are some of my oldest and dearest friends," Kenzie said. "This is the Tiara Squad." The light touch of her nails sunk through his jacket. If Kenzie was forcing a smile, he couldn't tell. She beamed from ear to ear. Unlike the other women who rushed over to greet her, Kenzie's makeup and long lashes all seemed natural. The foreheads on some of the other ladies didn't even move when they screamed. Damn Botox. The other women also sported another type of bling on their fingers—some wedding rings and others engagement rings.

Ramon tried not to choke on his laughter but failed.

Kenzie elbowed him in the stomach. "Ouch, sorry. It's a pleasure to meet you all. Tiara Squad, eh?"

"With Kenzie as our leader," said the woman named British. It was the only name he remembered because of its distinctness.

Kenzie looped her arm around British's shoulder and bumped her hip. "Oh, be quiet."

"Brit," began one of the two blonde girls, "don't get Kenzie upset. I can't do squats in these Spanx."

"So Ramon," said the other blonde woman, "how do you know our captain?"

"Captain?" Ramon asked, raising a curious brow toward his date. "I knew you were a cheerleader, but captain?"

"You couldn't tell by her bossiness?" This time the bride, Felicia Ward-Crawford, came over to hug the ladies. Kenzie and her friends all fawned over her with another round of screams.

Felicia smiled in approval at Ramon. "And who is this plus-one your Auntie Bren was telling me about back at the church?"

Kenzie made another set of introductions to the bride and her groom, Gary Crawford, who now walked over to the group.

"Kenzie came through for me last summer when she coordinated a pageant that was held at my hotel," Ramon said. He glanced over and winked at Kenzie.

"Magnolia Palace?" British leaned forward.

"You own Magnolia Palace?" a slender brunette asked with eyes wide in disbelief.

"You had Kenzie Swayne working at Magnolia Palace?" asked the blonde.

"And you're still alive?" British rested her arm on Kenzie's shoulder.

"Y'all leave him alone." Kenzie laughed, pushing British's hand off her shoulder.

Ramon took a step backward and watched Kenzie in her element. Last summer she coordinated the whole pageant at Magnolia Palace. After standing her up for the party after the pageant, Ramon hadn't seen a lot of Kenzie—at least not in her element. Last weekend Ramon had felt her tension from being around her family. Right now Kenzie's smile was genuine and happy. Another lady came over to the group and whispered in the bride's and groom's ears.

"Y'all, we all have to get upstairs," announced Felicia. "Kenzie, I insist you walk in with us. It just wouldn't be the same."

As if looking to him for permission, Kenzie cocked her brow at Ramon. He nodded his head and watched the members of the Tiara Squad squeeze themselves into one of the elevators. Through the glass he could see her full lips spread into a genuine smile, which caused Ramon's heart to twinge. *Hmph*, he thought to himself, *that was an odd feeling*. Ramon didn't think he was the type of person with a closed, cold heart. But he also didn't think he'd be the type of person whose heart skipped at the sight of a smile.

"You might as well come upstairs and get a drink with me."

Ramon looked to his left and came eye to eye with Alexander Ward. Ramon thought he'd recognized him as one of the groomsmen at the altar and now extended his hand for a shake. "Mr. City Manager."

The second set of elevators opened up and the two men entered. "You say it as if I have some authority." Alexander chuckled and pressed the button to the top floor. "Right this way."

Alexander nodded and pointed toward the bar in the back of the restaurant in front of the floor to ceiling windows. A pretty bartender entertained the best men with bottle tosses.

Women stopped the city official along the way and, judging from how they reached out for a hug or an air kiss, Ramon pegged him a player. But still Ramon followed. He needed a drink. He needed something to take his mind off how devastatingly gorgeous Kenzie was in her dress and how he almost hadn't let her put it on this evening.

"What are you having?" Alexander asked.

"Any Torres Rum?"

Alexander's face broke out in a grin. "Of course. We have nothing but the best for my twin sister."

"Twins?" Ramon repeated.

Alexander lifted his finger to catch the bartender and gave the man their order. "So how's the research on the building going?"

Ramon looked across the room where he left Kenzie. "It's going fine. I learned from Kenzie's memos that brick lasts one hundred years and that it's overdue for a makeover, which is not something a new buyer wants to deal with."

"We have a great construction company in town," said Alexander, "and we've also partnered up with the surrounding cities at Four Points. Good pricing, too."

"I'm okay with paying," Ramon said, twisting his lips together in thought. "I want to make sure this is understood for anyone else interested. Maybe warn them off."

"You don't think I'd cut Erin Hairston the same deal?" Alexander asked.

Ramon took a swig of his drink and studied the man over the rim of his glass. Did the man think he'd put pressure on Ramon to make a quick sale? Or was Alexander working an angle to get benefits with the contractors? He figured he'd get with Nate, a licensed carpenter, at some point to get an estimate. There was something to be said about buying locally but Ramon trusted family.

"So I thought I saw you come down to City Hall this week."

"You did." The bartender set two glasses in front of them. Both reached for one to take.

"I hope you were able to find what you needed."

The way his drinking partner said it, Ramon wondered if he meant more. Ramon followed the man's stare across the room to the exact spot where Kenzie and her friends were. He wondered which one he was interested in.

"I found what I wanted," said Ramon.

He was up there dropping off some of the ballots he'd scooped up from the basement. In the ruckus of being rescued a week ago, Ramon had left the other items from the closet. At City Hall Ramon found a specialist who'd said it would take a couple of weeks to figure out the slips' dates and coordinate them with what was going on in town at the time. He hated to admit Kenzie's enthusiasm infected him. He hoped the analysis of results on the age of the paper came in before the sesquicentennial. His parents, Ana and Julio Torres, planned on coming and Ramon wanted more than anything to prove to his parents he could make a life outside of Villa San Juan without the help of his family connections. He wanted to show them he contributed and belonged in Southwood, just as his ancestors did in VSJ. Buying Magnolia Palace was just a start.

"It's good to see Kenzie out and about," Alexander said all of a sudden.

Though the statement was out of the blue, Ramon squelched his curiosity by taking another swig. Like Villa San Juan, everyone in Southwood grew up with each other and many were probably related. Ramon recalled some of the names from his history lesson of Southwood. Four major families helped pull the city together, the Swaynes, Hairstons, Pendergrasses and Wards. Ramon drained his drink and nodded, realizing these two must have gone way back.

"Better seeing her with you than with that other dude she drags to all her functions," Alexander went on. "It's just interesting to see her taste in men since we broke up."

Ramon controlled himself to stop from turning and punching this jerk in the face. Was he seriously going to either sell him some property or throw away the deal? Clearly the man was insecure. Given the beauty on the dance floor, Ramon thought, casting a glance at Kenzie, he understood. He wondered how the two of them worked around each other. No wonder Kenzie was in a perpetual bad mood whenever Alexander came around. This was also the second time this murderer Kenzie dated had been mentioned. He wasn't sure what bothered him more, the fact she dated a killer or the fact she dated other people at all. A woman like Kenzie wouldn't wait around for a man like him to come around and make up his mind.

Ramon leaned his back against the edge of the bar. Even though this was Felicia's wedding reception, Kenzie stood in the center of the dance floor in a circle with the bridesmaids, her friends and the bride, laughing and having a good time. Ramon liked the way her head tilted backward. She wore her hair down and kept the long ringlets tamed. Each defined curl sparkled under the strobe lights. Kenzie swayed and shimmied her hips. Her shoulders twisted and bumped against her friend standing next to her as they belted out the lyrics to the song playing. Ramon wanted more than anything to be a part of Kenzie's life right now. The trendy pop song the ladies danced to blended into a Latin trumpet beat.

"Oh, how I love this song."

Ramon glanced down beside him at a feminine form. Auntie Bren, decked out in a royal purple gown and a set of jewels wrapped around her neck to complete the regal look, set her glass of champagne down on the bar top.

"Would you care to dance?" Alexander asked.

The sweet smile Ramon knew Auntie Bren to normally sport faded. "Not with you."

Alexander smiled awkwardly. "She's playing hard to get," he explained to Ramon.

"Not with him," said Auntie Bren. "Ramon, grant an old lady a wish and take her out on the dance floor."

"You have to point me in the direction of an old lady," Ramon teased and took hold of Auntie Bren's hand to lead her to the dance floor.

"Thank you for saving me back there," Auntie Bren said, settling her arms on his shoulders.

Two ladies in one week, Ramon thought to himself. He wasn't surprised his dance partner kept up the tempo so when he felt the time was right to dip her, he did. He just didn't expect Kenzie to almost bump heads with her great-aunt when the elderly man she was dancing with dipped her.

Auntie Bren gripped Ramon's biceps to pull herself up and clung to his shoulders. "Oh dear, there's Oscar Blakemore."

Ramon followed Auntie Bren's glare. "Boyfriend?"

"Hush," she hissed, swatting Ramon's chest. "He wishes."

The Blakemore man stared at them through the crowd toward them. Even though he walked with a cane, Mr. Blakemore didn't let that stop him from barreling onto the dance floor, shouldering people along his way. The song ended. Just as Ramon reached for Auntie Bren's fingertips to apply a thankful kiss, a heavy hand slammed against the side of his shoulder. Ramon knew exactly what to expect—a showdown for Auntie Bren's honor. Shoulders squared, Ramon prepared for battle. The old man's pinched lips sneered, then it was blurred. Kenzie's beautiful face came into focus.

"There you are," Kenzie cooed. "Auntie Bren, you don't mind if I steal my date away now, do you?"

Immediately Auntie Bren nodded her head. Her eyes were focused on the challenger. "Not at all."

"This will allow me the opportunity to keep you company on the dance floor," Mr. Blakemore said, extending his elbow.

Beside him, Kenzie pushed Ramon's arm.

"What?"

"Mr. Blakemore is a decorated veteran and a former boxer."

"Okay?" Ramon asked slowly and then a story clicked in his head. "So that's Auntie Bren's two-timing boyfriend from back in the day?"

"Stop calling her that," Kenzie huffed. "He also could have knocked you out with one punch or with his cane."

Ramon wrapped his arms around Kenzie's waist and drew her against his body. "First you're worried about my hotel competition and now my health. This is the best date ever."

"I never agreed it was a date."

Ramon dipped his head and lowered his mouth to hers for a kiss that tasted of champagne. The Tiara Squad made a bunch of ohhing and ahhing noises. "Too late—you already claimed me to Auntie Bren."

"Stop calling…" Kenzie bit her bottom lip and shook her head. She rose up on her heels and pulled him down to her. "Aw, hell, never mind."

Chapter 7

Kenzie hated to be embarrassed, but kissing Ramon on the dance floor should have been at the top of her charts for embarrassing moments, but it wasn't. Maybe because her friends, including the bride, cheered her on for finally succumbing to his charms. The DJ in the corner played a slow song; Kenzie didn't know which. She barely heard the beat over her own heart thumping in her chest. The crystal ball flickered light across Ramon's face. He smiled down at her.

"I'm digging this PDA," he teased. "What's wrong with it?"

The rhythm of the song set in as Kenzie pressed her forehead against the center of Ramon's ribs. Her stilettos helped balance the height difference between them. "I don't like the spotlight on me."

"Says the beauty queen." Ramon laughed, moving his hand from around her waist to tilt her chin toward him.

"Pageants are different." Kenzie rolled her eyes. "I am proud of my tiara."

Ramon shook his head and blew out a sigh. "What am I? Chopped liver?"

"I mean, I'm proud of holding my title as the last Swayne or Hairston—don't get me wrong," she boasted. "But that's as much of my business as I want to let people in on."

"People in town know about the guy you were dating?"

"Clearly you want to know about my dating history."

"You don't have to tell me," said Ramon, stiffening.

"I'll tell you this one time." Kenzie moved her hands to grip Ramon's biceps. She tried not to pay attention to how solid he felt and how weak her grip was. "Rafe is an old friend of mine. His wife died a few years ago and he was under heavy suspicion."

"Define 'heavy'?"

"While he was away serving our country, she was having several affairs. Rafe came back and found out but according to him he didn't even care."

Ramon snorted. "Didn't care?"

"No," Kenzie said with a shrug. "He'd been in love with another woman for a long time, so I guess his feelings weren't too hurt and he wanted a divorce. So anyway, Fourth of July night, Rafe came home to a bloody scene and no body. He was questioned."

"Did he have an alibi?"

"He told me he did," she answered, recalling the story Rafe had told her. Rafe didn't want to give up his alibi because of the person he was with wasn't fully divorced either. He protected the woman he loved. What had made Kenzie's relationship perfect with Rafe was that his heart belonged to another woman. At least now that lady had come to her senses. And Kenzie was happy for her friend.

Though the music continued, Ramon stopped dancing. "And you're going to tell me you believe him."

Something about the tone in his voice irked Kenzie. It seemed like he didn't believe her or was mocking her.

Kenzie took a step backward. She had shared a personal story about her dearest friend and he was mocking her. A piece of Kenzie's heart ached. "Yes I believe him. Rafe at least comes through for my events."

"And there are so many events," Ramon said, exasperated. "You dragged me to at least a half dozen of them."

The corners of Kenzie's eyes twitched. She blinked in disbelief. Did he seriously just make fun of her? "What?"

"I'm just saying you're standing here gushing about some other guy for taking you to all these things, yet he's not here," said Ramon. "If he were such a standup kind of guy, why isn't he here now holding you? I miss one of your many parties that you planned and I'm exiled to hell and this guy stands you up for your month of stress and you place him on some sort of pedestal."

Kenzie took a step away from Ramon's embrace. "You know what." Kenzie's voice rose with anger. A couple dancing nearby stopped and looked at them. "Never mind," she said, lowering her voice. "I knew there was a reason I never trust you with anything."

"What? Wait, what's happening here?"

"Bye, Ramon."

Kenzie stormed past Ramon, bumping his shoulder in the process. Walking away was the best thing to do right now. She'd been a fool to think he'd changed. Kenzie rushed over to her table and grabbed her blue clutch and stormed out through the doors toward the elevator. She jammed her finger from pressing the button so hard.

"Running away from another man?"

Without having to turn around, Kenzie rolled her eyes at the sound of Alexander's voice. The ice in his beverage clanked against the glass. "Go away, Alexander."

"I can't go anywhere right now," said Alexander. "I'm too infatuated with you. You're gorgeous in that dress."

His speech sounded a bit slurred but it was no concern of Kenzie's. She pressed the already lit button to the elevator again and tucked her purse under her arm. Alexander approached. Rum seeped through his pores. She sighed in annoyance.

"Did you ever stop to think that this could be our wedding?" Alexander went on.

As if choking, Kenzie began to cough. Alexander stepped closer. "What do you say we get ourselves a room and pretend we're on our honeymoon? For old time's sake?"

The heat of his breath sent a twitch of fear down her spine. Alexander wasn't a vicious man but he was lecherous when drunk. Before she had a chance to say another word, Alexander made a yelp-like noise. The elevator arrived with a ding and she didn't bother turning around to give her ex a second thought. She needed to focus on the ride down. Damn Brutti Hotel, Kenzie thought. She rolled her eyes and slowly turned around just in time to watch Ramon give Alexander an odd side hug. Alexander's eyes widened as his cheek began to swell. Kenzie's darted her glare between Ramon and Alexander.

"Thanks for the directions, buddy," Ramon said, all chipper.

Kenzie's eyes scanned the odd way Ramon held his left fist. He kept opening and closing his fingers together.

"Going down?" Ramon asked. The doors sealed closed but didn't keep out Alexander's vulgar goodbye.

"Following me?" Kenzie asked, leveling her eyes with Ramon's. She willed her libido to settle down. Memories of their little afternoon excursion flooded her mind. Her heart raced with the memory of his touch. Damn him.

"Considering you're my date this evening…" he began and pressed the PL button for the plaza level.

Knees locked, Kenzie frowned. "We can cut the charade between us."

"I don't think so." Ramon turned his back to her for a moment and screwed around with one of the buttons. The hydraulics in the small compartment bounced to a stop. Kenzie accidently dropped her purse. "You have the nerve to walk away from me after you stood there gushing over some other man while we're on a date."

"I wasn't…" Kenzie tried to justify herself. "I tried to tell you…"

"About how great some other dude is?"

Judging from his flattened lips, Ramon recalled what she'd said. "I didn't."

"You think it was easy standing there and listening to you go on about Mr. Perfect?"

Bubbling laughter stirred in her sternum. "You're jealous?"

"Nah. I just don't appreciate it." Ramon folded his arms across his broad chest.

The male ego, Kenzie mused. Men didn't want what they had until someone else started playing with it. What made Ramon any different than Alexander? Alexander busied himself with other women back in college. Ten years had gone by and he never gave Kenzie a second thought. Now all of a sudden there was a spark on the dance floor with Ramon and he had something to say? Ramon hadn't given Kenzie so much thought in almost a year and the moment she talked about another guy he became jealous.

"What happened to your hand?" Kenzie asked, noticing his red knuckles.

"Alexander fell."

"On your fist?"

Ramon shrugged. "He was advancing toward you as you were getting on a small, confined elevator."

The reminder of where she was caused Kenzie to gulp. "Alexander is a bad drunk, but he's harmless. Can you start the elevator back up, please?"

"And you know this about Alexander because he's your ex?" Ramon asked without budging.

"Yeah, like when we were in high school. What does it matter?"

"It doesn't," said Ramon.

"Ramon, please start the elevator back up." Impatient, Kenzie stepped closer to him and tried to push the button. She had no idea which one he used to stop the elevator so she pressed them all. The compartment lowered a foot and bounced back up, then not only stopped but the lights also went out. The jolt sent Kenzie into Ramon's arms. "What just happened?"

"You broke the elevator," Ramon teased. "I'm kidding—there must be a short or something. Hang on."

He tried to let her go to turn to the panel but Kenzie clung to him. "Found the phone. Hello? Hello?"

With her hand still on his shoulders, Kenzie felt his lungs sink with a sigh. "What's wrong?"

"I can't get a person to pick up the phone."

"Are you serious?" Kenzie shrieked. "This stupid hotel and its cheap elevator."

"In the hotel's defense, you were pressing a lot of buttons, Kenzie."

Kenzie wanted to dig deep for the anger from earlier. Nothing came. She tried to find something else to be mad at. Better mad than what threatened. "Are you blaming me?" Kenzie inhaled and squared her shoulders.

"Relax," Ramon said, reaching for her. "Someone will come looking for us soon."

"Not likely," Kenzie huffed. "They were getting ready to serve dinner. Free bar and delicious food—no one is going to leave the reception hall any time soon."

"So that's good news for us."

Good for who? she thought. There was nothing Kenzie could do. If she peered against the glass she would succumb to her fear of falling, given how far up they were from the ground. Thanks to the hotel being built in a wooded area, the tops of the trees blocked her view from below. If she stood closer to Ramon, she'd give in to her fear of making love to him right here and now.

"Ever notice every other time we ride the elevator we get stuck?" Ramon teased in the darkness.

The starlit skyline filled the glass compartment. Kenzie wasn't sure which was worse—facing death if the elevator fell or facing Ramon. She took a chance on the latter and was greeted by a smirk across his face. "I am glad you can find the humor in this."

"Humor or opportunity?" he asked, feeling for her hand. The pad of his index finger stroked across the vein in her wrist.

Kenzie's pulse quickened with the touch. She wondered if he felt it, too. "Ramon, I don't think…"

"For once in your life, don't think," Ramon ordered her before reaching for the back of her neck with his large, warm hands. He cupped her neck with his fingers. His thumbs outlined her lips before his mouth came down to claim hers. For the second time this evening Kenzie's heart melted. Knees caving, she leaned into him. With one swoop Ramon lifted her by the bottom and wrapped her legs around his waist. With her back against the glass of the elevator the hem of her skirt rolled up her thighs. Neither of them broke their kiss. Kenzie fumbled with his belt buckle, which prevented her from touching him. She slid the leather from the loops and let it hit the floor with a clank. Nervously her fingers played with the button and zipper of his pants. She peeled away the material until she found what she was looking for.

The hard erection sprang to life in her hands. Kenzie groaned while she caressed the full length of him. A shiver of anticipation crept down her spine. Ramon tugged at the stitches of her panties until they ripped. He broke the kiss for a moment.

"I'll buy you a new pair," he growled, tucking the material into the inside pocket of his jacket. His hands pressed between her legs and fit her body onto him.

They both sucked in a deep breath at their connection. Kenzie wrapped her legs tighter around his waist. Ramon cupped her from under her arms and over her shoulder. He pulled her down onto him as his hips bucked forward.

Kenzie, filled with Ramon inside of her, wrapped her legs tighter. She arched her back and used the glass to help her sink deeper onto him. She gasped when Ramon tugged down her bodice and freed her breasts. Liquid desire coursed through her veins with the heat of his tongue across her nipples. Kenzie cried in ecstasy. Ramon pumped into her, fusing their bodies together. His fingers hung on to her shoulders. Her nails sunk into the fabric of his shirt.

"Ramon," she cried.

"Kenzie," he replied against her ear. His velvety voice against her lobe coaxed every ounce of orgasm out of her. She squeezed her legs around his waist, climbing him, grinding him until waves of pleasure poured from their bodies.

"Oh my God," Kenzie groaned into Ramon's neck. "I can't believe we did this."

Ramon planted a kiss on her forehead. His hands

roamed her thighs as he eased her back to her feet. "Believe it. And this isn't going to be the last time, either."

"We aren't getting back together," Kenzie announced. She found her shoes and slipped them back on, giving her a little bit more height next to Ramon.

A deep laughter filled the space between them. "See, there's your mistake." Ramon cupped Kenzie's face. "You keep looking at us as a couple last summer."

"I forgot, I was just a fling for you," Kenzie blurted out.

"Not a fling," clarified Ramon. "We were just getting to know each other."

"And what have you learned about me?" Kenzie asked.

The pads of his thumbs traced circles around her cheekbones. "I know you love your city. You love your family, and I know you hate being embarrassed."

Kenzie pulled her head away from his touch. "Do you know why I hate being embarrassed?"

"Because you're a perfectionist?"

Scoffing, Kenzie gripped the railing behind her. "I was engaged."

"Okay?" He tucked his shirt into his pants.

"To Alexander." Kenzie waited for another slow *okay* from Ramon as he fumbled with his belt. She expected to hear the jingle of the buckle. When he didn't respond at all she continued. "We were just out of high school and starting college. I thought I knew him but clearly everyone else did, too—both in town and on campus. When I joined him at school I was humiliated when everyone in my dorm had already been with him and when I came home mortified, everyone who tried to comfort me knew all about his ways."

Finally Ramon cleared his throat. He reached for her, draping his heavy arm over her shoulder. His fingers splayed against the nape of her neck. "You don't like being the butt of a joke but you don't mind being the center of attention." The last part came out with a chuckle.

"Shut up." Kenzie laughed.

"Kenzie," he said, reaching for her hands to bring to his lips. "I would never knowingly do something to embarrass you again."

A grinding noise sounded as Kenzie tried to gather her thoughts. The lights flickered a few times before deciding to stay on and the elevator began its descent down to the plaza floor.

"Here we go," Ramon said with a wink.

Kenzie pressed her hands to her face and pinched her cheeks. She must look a mess right about now. The reflection on the doors showed her hair was wild, but that was nothing new. The once-defined curls had their own sense of direction. The flowers of her bodice were crushed and her dress was wrinkled. When the elevator's doors slid open and a gush of air swept through, Kenzie was reminded of the absence of her panties. As if reading her mind Ramon patted the breast pocket of his jacket and cleared his throat.

Three men in maroon jackets met the two of them at the door. Apologies spilled from their mouths.

"Yes, we are extremely sorry for the inconvenience." A man, close to six five, dressed in a dark suit and with a turquoise carnation in his lapel, stepped forward. His black hair was cut short and parted on the side. He belonged on the cover of a magazine, not as a bellboy at a hotel, Kenzie thought. "Ramon?"

"Gianni?"

"Brutti?" Kenzie repeated and then snorted in disgust. Because of the location of the hotel, no one ever consulted with her about building it. Had Kenzie met Gianni Brutti in person, well, she still would have hated the idea of such an eyesore sticking out of the forest in Four Points Park, but she might not have hated looking at the man. Talk about eye candy.

"Ramon, you beautiful bastard," Gianni said in a booming voice. The men hugged and shook hands in that male bonding ritual Kenzie had seen football players do. "Had I known the competition was in my hotel spying, I might have let you stay in there longer."

"Man, what are you talking about? You aren't any competition." Ramon laughed, took a step back and wrapped his arm around Kenzie's waist. "Gianni, I'd like you to meet Kenzie Swayne. Kenzie, this is an old family friend, Gianni Brutti."

Gianni extended his hand and Kenzie, remembering her manners, returned the shake. "Pleased to meet you."

"Kenzie Swayne," Gianni repeated her name. "As in *the* Kenzie Swayne, of the Swaynes of Southwood."

"The one and only." Ramon beamed.

"Your beauty surpasses the photographs, Miss Southwood."

Kenzie rolled her eyes. "What?"

"I have a wedding reception going on upstairs. The bride insisted on having photographs posted upstairs," answered Gianni. "Didn't you two see them?"

"We were kind of busy," said Ramon.

Gianni leaned forward and shook Ramon's hand again. Kenzie watched the way Ramon's cheeks rose in a silent laugh at whatever the man said to him. "Thanks, man," Ramon replied. "Well, we'll see you around."

"Most definitely," said Gianni. "Your mother told me she's made reservations here for the sesquicentennial in Southwood next week."

"Funny. See you later." Ramon escorted Kenzie outside to where he parked his car.

"What was that all about?"

Ramon cast a glance toward the hotel. "What? My folks? I'm sure he was joking. I've had reservations held for my family for weeks now."

"What did he whisper to you?" Kenzie asked.

"Oh, that? Well, let's just say I have already started keeping my promise to you." Ramon opened the passenger door and allowed Kenzie the chance to sit first. She climbed in but kept staring, waiting for his answer. "Let's just say the lights were off but the cameras were still rolling. Gianni is going to erase everything for us."

It hadn't been Ramon's intent, but he woke Kenzie up the next morning by accidently kicking open the door to her bedroom. Last night, instead of walking Kenzie to her apartment door, he'd stayed, continuing what they did in the elevator. And he was glad he had, too, except for the fact he had no clothes other than his dress slacks to change into. In his defense, carrying a breakfast tray filled with a wineglass of orange juice, a bottle of water, two egg-white omelets, toast and two bowls of fresh peaches was a struggle. He made a mental note to give the staff at Magnolia Palace a raise for making it look so easy.

Upon the clumsy entrance, Kenzie sat up in the bed. One side of her hair fell across the left side of her shoulder, covering her bare breast. She brought the pink comforter to her neck in an attempt to be modest.

"Nah," Ramon said shaking his head. He set the make-shift tray on the edge of her bed and reached for the covers to expose her luscious body. "Too late to be bashful now."

Kenzie gave him a lazy smile. "Yet you're so formal in your pants."

"Good thing you didn't have any bacon. I would have been forced to make it."

"No one would force you," Kenzie said with a laugh. She scooted over to make room at the head of the bed. She tucked her long, slender legs to sit crisscross applesauce style, as Philly used to say.

"Oh yes, if bacon is in a refrigerator, it belongs in a frying pan—it's a law," said Ramon, trying to recall the last time he ever brought food or cooked breakfast for a woman in her home. He wondered what made her so special but when she cocked a brow at him, not believing his theory, he realized why. She didn't fall for his BS. "I'm a man—we are drawn to bacon."

"Maybe that's what my brother was doing in my fridge last week." Kenzie pondered, her finger on her chin. "Since he and Bailey moved back to town, he seems to do a lot of shopping from my kitchen."

"Your brother Richard?" Ramon asked, trying to recall meeting him at Corie's wedding last week.

"He has yet to learn that a woman is impressed by a man who cooks," Kenzie mused over the tray. "I'm impressed. Did you once tell me you have brothers?"

"Three of them," Ramon boasted.

Kenzie's pink lips parted for a whistle. "No sisters?"

"No, but we have cousins."

"Your poor mom."

"You mean poor me." Ramon laughed. "Being the youngest of four boys, six if you include how close me, Stephen and Nate are, I got beat up a lot."

"Aw, poor thing." Sincerity was lacking in her voice but because she was naked and eating his food, Ramon was not going to complain.

"That's all right." Ramon snagged the slice of peach off her fork. "My mama took care of me and fed me."

"Fed you what?"

"What *didn't* she feed me." Ramon chuckled. "I didn't always have this physique."

Kenzie took a peach off his plate. The ripe skin matched her nipples. Ramon stirred on his side of the bed.

"So you were a mama's boy?"

Holding his left hand in the air with his right over his heart, Ramon gave his oath. "I cannot tell a lie. It was pretty bad."

For the first time ever, Ramon confessed what it was like for him growing up. He spoke while keeping his focus on the sheets until Kenzie touched his kneecap. When he glanced up, their eyes met. He'd seen her with the kids at the wedding last night. She'd make a wonderful mother. If they ever had a child together, Ramon imagined Kenzie nurturing him and if their boy got teased, he wouldn't march his son back outside like his father did. "And yet you decided to leave the comfort of your mama's side to start anew here in Southwood."

Ramon reached out and ran his hand along her smooth thigh. "What a great decision that was, huh?"

"The jury is still out," Kenzie said with a roll of her eyes.

In a smooth swoop, Ramon pushed the tray farther to the edge of the bed with his legs and with his hands, lifted Kenzie onto his lap. Kenzie pressed her palms against his chest. He wondered if she felt the way his heart beat faster at the mere touch of her skin. "You can't possibly be thinking about going another round," she stated rather than asked.

Ramon's fingers were splayed on her naked hips. "Weren't you the one questioning my stamina last week?" He lifted his hips forward and cursed the restraining fabric of his pants. Ramon cocked his head to the side and kissed her lips. She tasted like peaches. Truth be told, he could go several rounds with Kenzie. He pushed her hair back and kissed her freckled shoulder.

"The food is getting cold," Kenzie moaned. The vibrations of her vocal chords tickled his lips.

"Fine," he said with a sigh, "I don't want you passing out on me when I ravish you later."

"Later?" Kenzie wedged her bottom between his opening thighs, resting her legs on top of his. He was drowning in unchartered infatuation. He had never felt this way with a woman before. He couldn't get enough of her. And the fact she looked at him like she felt the same way he felt drove him over the edge. Desire overcame him when she leaned backward, baring her breasts to him as she reached backward to drag the tray closer to the two of them. He willed himself to behave.

Oblivious, Kenzie continued what she was saying. "I have to meet up with Bailey down at Grits and Glam Gowns."

"Ah, you're going to see my family, Lexi?"

"Speaking of family," Kenzie began, pulling the crust off the buttered toast. Ramon watched with amusement, still waiting for her to finish her statement, while she meticulously pinched off any sign of crust. A red tint splashed across her face when she looked up and found him looking at her. "Crust makes your hair curly."

"I'm pretty sure that isn't true."

Kenzie tugged a few strands of her hair. "Want to make a bet?"

"No." Ramon chuckled.

"Back to your family," she said, poking her tongue out. "I am putting the seating charts together. Are you aware you have a table of twelve at the gala?"

"Yeah," he began with a tsk. "We're keeping it small.

Stephen and Nate's mom is coming to town for the afternoon festivities but she is going to babysit Philly."

The mention of his niece brought a smile to Kenzie's face. Since he assumed she wanted to be married, Ramon wondered where Kenzie stood on having children. He wondered why any of that mattered. Pushing the thought out of his mind, Ramon grabbed the discarded crusts and shoved them into his mouth. Crust spilled out when he tried to give her a toothy smile.

"Ew." She frowned. She lifted her hands to shake his hair out of the knot he put on the top of his head. "Now you're going to have curly hair."

"I don't care." Thanks to the bread in his mouth, his answer came out muffled.

"Now, what would your mother say?"

Chewing, Ramon grabbed the water bottle to wash it down. "I don't know. Let's call her." Ramon leaned back against the headboard and grabbed his phone from his pocket.

"Stop." Kenzie busted out laughing.

"I don't mind," Ramon said.

"I mind," she gasped. "What would your mother think of me if you called her at this hour?"

Ramon set his phone on the night stand. "Well, let's see…how am I going to introduce you?"

"Kenzie Swayne, Southwood historian."

"Okay, Kenzie Swayne, Southwood historian." Ramon mocked her and grinned when she poked her tongue out at him. One more time and he was going to capture it with his mouth. "We can tell my mother the same story we're telling Auntie Bren."

"Stop calling her…"

Ramon shoved a piece of fruit into Kenzie's mouth before she could finish. "Auntie Bren and I have bonded.

Before you took advantage of me last night I was playing the perfect wingman for her."

"I'm sure," Kenzie said after chewing for a moment, "she truly appreciates you helping her."

"I would do anything for her—that's my buddy." He meant it with all sincerity. Even though Ramon had left his large family, it was comforting being around a surrogate one like Kenzie's.

"So anyway," she huffed, "how do you plan on introducing me to your mother?"

"I like that you're eager to meet the family, Kenzie."

"Considering my family is convinced we're in some sort of relationship, I think it's only fair."

"'Some sort of'?" he repeated, feeling let down that this was not a permanent situation between them.

"Well, you know, this thing between us," Kenzie began, wagging her fingers between the two of them.

Ramon sat up and away from the headboard. "You mean my proposal, the one you refuse to give me an answer to?"

"Yet we've already been to two different events and lunch a few times last week."

Ramon shook his head. "Lunch was a work thing. And one of those meals we shared with your cousin Erin." Judging from her frown, Ramon confirmed Kenzie did not care for her family member. "What is the deal between you two?"

Her light shoulder shrug made the juice in the glass slosh. "It's silly, now that I think about it."

"Tell me."

"Erin and I are the same age and it seemed like we were always competing for everything growing up, including Auntie Bren's affection. Auntie Bren never cared for beauty pageants, which of course are in my blood."

"Miss Southwood." Ramon bowed his head.

"Please." Kenzie rolled her eyes. "Erin always said pageants were degrading for women."

"You don't agree?"

"Of course not. Pageants are not just a way of life in the South—they're such a confidence builder."

Ramon felt his eyes widen. "How so? There's only one winner and it's based on beauty."

The bottom portion of her succulent lip poked out. "You're judged on several things—beauty, talent and speech."

"No, someone has to walk away a loser." Ramon reached for her calf, smoothed his hand down to her foot and lifted it to kiss her big toe. As expected, she tried to pull away, but he kept a firm hold. "Don't," he warned. "Don't pull away because I don't agree."

Crossing her arms, Kenzie shook her head. "Not if you're going to sit here and make fun of me."

"I'm not making fun of you, just trying to understand how pageants build egos."

"You attended one last year."

"No, I came after the crowning," Ramon reminded her and then stopped himself. After the crowning, there had been that party that he didn't escort her to, which had landed him in months of torture from Kenzie. He never wanted to go down that road again. "Sorry," he said.

Knowing where the conversation was going, Kenzie offered a soft smile. "You're entitled to your own opinion."

"That means without retaliation?"

"I know nothing of which you speak." Kenzie played coy with him, hiding her laugh behind the glass of juice she picked up.

"I guess my truck getting towed and the salt being replaced with sugar at the food truck thing, and other little antics were just a coincidence?"

"You could look at it that way, or at least look at it like—" she paused and licked her lips "—if I didn't care, I probably wouldn't have felt the need to retaliate."

"Twisted." Ramon wiggled his eyebrows.

"Twisted is my flesh and blood rooting for my opponent."

"Your opponent being the woman whose wedding we attended yesterday evening?"

Kenzie nodded. "Felicia and I are friends. We will always be friends, but knowing Erin campaigned against me…" She shook her head. A curl fell over her shoulder. "That was betrayal."

"How could she campaign against you? Aren't there judges?"

"There used to be," Kenzie explained, "but in order to get people to come out to the pageant, you have to get supporters. Erin backed Felicia, even put money in toward her getting a gown and everything. But I still won," she boasted with a proud smile.

"Okay, I get it," he lied.

Eyes narrowing on him, Kenzie shook her head. "Do you really now?"

"No," he admitted. "I just like the way you smile when you talk about winning."

Once again Kenzie poked her tongue out at him. This time he pushed everything aside and kept the promise he made to himself, taking her once more.

Chapter 8

Instead of meeting up with Bailey and Lexi for a fitting the previous afternoon, Kenzie stayed in her apartment making love to Ramon all day long. All her life she'd prided herself on keeping her word and always being there for people. She woke up this morning kissing him good-bye so he could tend to the hotel as well as talk to some construction teams. If he planned on buying the old post office, it was going to need some work done to it.

When she strolled through the studio side of Grits and Glam Gowns, Kenzie expected to find Bailey highly disappointed in her. Kenzie was faced with four sets of inquiring eyes: Lexi's, Maggie's, Bailey's and Andrew Mason's. Andrew helped run and manage the dozens of toddlers who came to the studio for pageant lessons. At one point Lexi was the coach but with two small children and another on the way things were getting hectic.

Kenzie wrapped her arm around her niece's neck and hugged her. She smelled like Love's Baby Soft perfume and bubble gum. In a way, Kenzie wished Bailey would never grow up. Maybe this pageant wasn't a good idea. But pageants at seventeen and eighteen were a rite of passage.

Once Bailey won, Kenzie knew her baby niece would be all grown up. Next month she would be eighteen.

"I'm sorry for missing yesterday," Kenzie said as she tugged on the frayed hole in the knee of Bailey's jeans. Kenzie had realized that women over twenty-five didn't need to wear holey jeans anymore. She smoothed her hands down the backside of her loose-fitting black skirt and pulled down the hem of her black Grits and Glam Gowns T-shirt with the words Tiara Squad bedazzled in pink and white gems on the front.

Bailey sat on the edge of the black stage where numerous tap dancing lessons had been held over the years. After the hug she sat so her elbows were propped on her knees and her chin propped in her hands. Her big brown eyes blinked and her hair was in two long pigtails; guilt couldn't help but wash over Kenzie.

"I can't believe you forgot about me," Bailey said with a sniffle.

"I—I didn't forget," Kenzie exclaimed and glared at Maggie. "I told Aunt…" She stopped her accusation when everyone started laughing.

"Funny." Kenzie half laughed, half sneered at her sister, who wore a pair of denim short-shorts, a flowy cream-colored blouse and four-inch heels. The wide-brimmed hat on top of her head was obnoxious, Kenzie thought and then corrected herself. She loved the hat and planned on taking it from her sister one of these days.

"Sorry." Bailey held her hands up in surrender. "Auntie Maggie made me do it. I'm glad you're getting busy."

The comment threw Kenzie off for a moment. She scrunched up her eyes but Maggie garnered Kenzie's attention. Unashamed for using their niece to goad Kenzie into guilt, Maggie doubled over on the stage. "Your face."

"My finger," Kenzie sneered, flipping her sister off.

"Aren't you supposed to be some sort of socialite with at least an ounce of poise?"

"But first I am your older sister," Maggie said, sliding off the stage, "and tormenting you comes with the job."

Kenzie thought about her conversation with Ramon the other morning in bed and wondered if his brothers had ever teased him the way her sisters had her.

"Right," Kenzie said with a nod. "My much *older* sister."

"Hey, we're not talking about me here—we're talking about you," said Maggie. "What exactly were you doing yesterday?"

Kenzie cast a glance at Bailey. No way in the world she was going to discuss where or what or especially who she was doing in front of her niece. Almost eighteen or not.

"We should be discussing Bailey," Lexi suggested, fanning out her hot-pink shift dress. The material did not hide Lexi's full belly.

"Great idea," Kenzie and Bailey chorused.

Since the studio session was paid for, the group made the best of the situation. The morning ticked by. Kenzie tried to focus on her niece's dancing, but since the girl had every routine thrown at her down pat, rehearsals ended sooner. Chantal, Kenzie's cousin, was supposed to be the dance instructor at Grits and Glam Studios, but had left to live overseas with her husband; Andrew knew most of the routines and taught Bailey what he knew. Kenzie grinned to herself, remembering how she taught Ramon the pageant wave this morning.

"Bailey," Lexi began, "because you're so talented, I really think you can do your own ensemble, just take over the whole show. I was thinking something like 'Singing in the Rain.'"

"Except it hasn't rained in Southwood in weeks," Andrew reminded them. "How delightful are the judges going to find her number when they are sweating to death?"

"Are we doing it in the theater downtown?" Maggie asked. "That A/C has been spotty again."

Kenzie turned to her sister. "And you know this how?"

"I scoped it out in case I wanted to throw a party there."

"Seriously?" Kenzie scoffed.

"What? My friends have been in search of the small-town feel. No one can believe I'm from here."

"Lexi," Kenzie whined, "don't bring your partying friends to Southwood."

"My partying friends like to spend money, Kenzie."

"Can the two of you stop fighting?" Andrew asked, fanning himself with his hand. "We need to concentrate on Bailey."

"Yeah," Bailey chimed in. "Although I'm not sure about the singing and dancing. What if I get winded?"

"You ran track last semester," said Kenzie. "You will be fine."

They went over the number a few times. Kenzie liked it but she wasn't sold. Given the way Lexi sat, looking pained and uncomfortable, she didn't think she wanted to let her mentor know how worried. An hour into rehearsal, Kenzie sat back in the couch, which was shaped like a pair of lips and set against the window. Break couldn't have come at a better time. Bailey went to check her phone. When the clock in the tower downtown struck twelve, Andrew went off to get some food for them before rehearsal started back up again.

Their afternoon would be given to Bailey's vocal coach, Waverly Crowne. Waverly, last year's Miss Southwood, was a shoo-in for the Miss Georgia Pageant but had found out Christmas Eve she'd had a better title to achieve: that of Mrs. Dominic Crowne. They were already married and expecting their first child but they'd been married in a hurry, and the wedding was largely for Waverly's mother's sake. So far, Waverly hasn't discovered her husband's plans for a second, secret wedding. Waverly was still acting as a vocal coach for all the pageants for toddlers and little kids; fortunately this included Bailey. Thank God the Miss Southwood pageant was the Saturday after next.

A surge of electricity coursed through Kenzie at the idea of the month almost being over. She shifted on the cushions of the red couch. Already two events in and she was sleeping with Ramon. *Again.* How weak did that make her? She was a repeat offender or something. Last summer it hadn't taken long for her to sleep with him, either. This time around things felt different. Ramon shared things with her. When he told her about his childhood, she felt his pain.

Lexi waddled toward the couch and Kenzie got up from her corner to help. Maggie leaped from her perch on the couch, as well, also to aid Lexi down to the cushion.

Lexi swatted her hands in the air. "I've got this."

Stepping back, Kenzie bit the corner of her thumbnail. She wondered where Stephen was and didn't recall seeing his car. Stephen owned Southwood's finest real estate agency, located right next door to Grits and Glam Gowns. If Lexi went into labor now, she wasn't sure what to do.

A loud "Oh my God" penetrated the glass wall looking out onto the street. Bailey stood, talking with someone on the other end of her phone via FaceTime.

"For a girl who didn't want to move to Southwood because she didn't have any friends here," Kenzie noted, watching Bailey, "she certainly is a busybody."

Maggie bowed at her hip. "She's just like her Auntie Maggie."

"God help her," Kenzie groaned.

"Don't worry too much," said Lexi, waddling over to them. "She's adjusting fine and making tons of friends."

"Speaking of making friends," Maggie began, knocking her knees against Kenzie's, "we haven't seen you since Felicia's wedding reception."

Heat bubbled under the collar of Kenzie's shirt.

"She doesn't have to answer," Lexi teased. "Just look at the glow on her face."

"My glow," Kenzie repeated. "Lexi, I'm really worried about you. Are you sure you don't want to go home for the day?"

"No, because if Stephen gets wind that I'm sweaty the man is going to put me on bed rest for the rest of this pregnancy. I have another six weeks."

Kenzie doubted her friend was going to make it that long, but she wasn't going to say anything.

"Let's get back to you and Ramon," Maggie persisted.

"Let's not."

"Stephen said you drove out to the hotel last week," said Lexi, entertaining Maggie's choice of topics.

"And I thought I saw the two of you having lunch in the park," added Maggie.

Although it was none of their business, Kenzie explained how she ended up with Ramon's jacket the night of Corie's wedding. "And if you saw me having lunch in the park with Ramon, you must have just missed Erin. She wants to purchase the post office also."

"What?" Lexi and Maggie chorused.

Kenzie shook her head. "I know, shocking, isn't it? She wants to turn it into a clinic."

"They have that sports center in Orlando," commented Maggie. "Why?"

"Erin hates the tranquility of Southwood." Kenzie

snorted. "She couldn't wait to get out of here because she hated how small and quiet things were."

"Ugh," Maggie groaned. "How will her proposal go over with the council?"

The city council planned on meeting this week. Kenzie already knew she wouldn't recommend Erin's proposal—not out of spite but because if she had her clients here, most of whom were professional athletes, it would disrupt the tranquility of Southwood.

As she told the ladies her decision, Maggie cocked her head to the side and moaned. "Now there's a disturbance for you."

Kenzie followed Maggie's line of sight. Her heart thumped when she found Ramon standing behind her with two coffee cups in his hands. He wore a black tank top, ballers and earbuds in his ears. His hair hung loose around his neck. Behind him Bailey held her phone up...no doubt Kenzie expected to find the photo on social media later.

"Are you ogling him?" Kenzie asked. She waved Ramon in and pushed away from the couch to greet him.

"Jealous?" Maggie called out to her.

"Ladies," Ramon boomed, walking through the studio's side doors.

Stephen, dressed similarly to Ramon, came in through the kitchenette area between the studio and the dress shop side. "It's time for a break."

"We're already taking a break, Stephen," Lexi said. "See?" She fanned her hand down the length of her seated body.

Once reaching his wife, Stephen sat on the armrest and dipped his head for a kiss. The kiss lingered longer than anyone wanted to witness. Ramon cleared his throat.

"Uh, isn't that what got your wife in the situation she's in now?" Ramon asked.

"I can't wait for you to fall in love," Stephen retorted.

Another pang clenched Kenzie's heart. The idea of Ramon falling in love with anyone else didn't go over well with her. She cleared her throat to keep her feelings in check. Ramon remembered the coffee cups in his hand.

"Hey, I almost forgot, this is for you." He handed her the beverage. Warmth touched her hands. "Cream and two sugars."

Kenzie smiled but Maggie gaped. "And how exactly do you know how my sister likes her coffee?"

"Café con leche?" Ramon replied. "Who doesn't like their coffee like that?"

The answer didn't set well with Maggie. She narrowed her eyes on them. "I don't believe you, but since you said it with an accent, I'm going to let it go." She waltzed over to the record table and thumbed through the collection. Bailey came in and went over to Maggie.

"Did we interrupt anything?" Ramon asked Kenzie.

"Just taking a break for lunch," said Kenzie. "Bailey's been working hard all morning on her routine."

"And you've been sitting down?" Stephen asked Lexi.

"Of course."

Stephen gave his wife's arm a loving stroke. "Good. Cinderella over here is trying to kill me. Her feet get puffy if she stands on her feet too long."

Kenzie glanced up at Ramon, who hid his laugh behind his cup and gave her a wink. "You guys were just playing basketball, right?"

"Yes," Stephen said with a nod, "I'm not sure if he had a chance to tell you but my little cousin here used to be well over on the husky side."

All Ramon had alluded to was that his mother plied him with sweets as a kid. Looking at him now she found it hard to believe he'd had any weight issues. The man was pure muscle.

"We're not talking about me," Ramon reminded his cousin.

"Hey, Kenzie," Maggie called out, "Lexi has the song from your routine when you ran for Miss Southwood."

Kenzie cut her eyes at Lexi, who shrugged innocently. "It's a classic song."

"What song is it?" Stephen and Ramon asked together.

Kenzie continued to stare at Lexi, willing her not to say a word.

"Mambo," Maggie replied. "Or at least it was the mambo scene from *West Side Story*."

Beside her, Kenzie felt Ramon's blaze of heat. "Seriously? Do you have any video? Please say there's video."

"No." Kenzie shook her head.

"Do you remember your steps, Auntie?" Bailey asked, using her pleading, sad, puppy-dog eyes. "I need all the inspiration I can get."

Maggie headed toward the record player. "You know it's one of those songs with a beat Kenzie can't resist."

"I can resist," said Kenzie, willing her body to stay still. "Besides, my dance partner isn't here."

Bailey's eyes lit up. "Who was your dance partner?"

"Hank DuVernay," Kenzie replied over the beginning of the song, "and there's no way…"

Andrew, carrying two boxes of pizza, set their lunch on the stage. "Anything my ex can do, I can do better." He swiveled his satin scarf from around his neck to the rhythm of the bongo-driven beat of the song. Ramon took the cup of coffee from Kenzie's hand. Lexi, Bailey and Maggie egged Kenzie on with catcalls and whistles.

Something took over Kenzie, just as the spirit of Rita Moreno had taken her over when she competed for Miss

Southwood. By the time the song finished, people waiting for the afternoon music lesson were gathered around the doors of the studios and folks pressed their faces to the window for the show. Breathless, Kenzie beamed and bowed to Andrew for dancing with her. He was better than Hank. As the people gathered on the studio floor, Kenzie glanced around to find Ramon. Just as Maria and Tony had found each other on the dance floor, he made his way to her. Chest heaving, Kenzie looked away, not sure if her interpretation of the Puerto Rican dance queen was accurate or not. Ramon approached with confidence; he took Kenzie by the arms and spun her around, dipping her backward.

"You're wearing this and doing that exact same dance tonight."

With her hair pulled back into a French twist and armed with her seersucker jacket, Kenzie, well-rehearsed in the speech she planned on giving in a few minutes, confidently pushed away from her desk. She wore a pair of seersucker Capri pants and black high-heeled sandals and felt like a million bucks. Then the back of her chair hit the wall, putting her ego in check. The fancy degree she earned didn't give her a corner office and six-figure salary and so far the only historical fact Kenzie discovered going through the old yearbooks was that Southwood High had a winning football team. The nerves kicked in.

Kenzie paused for a moment and sighed to push her fears away. She hated speaking in front of people. Even at beauty pageants, Kenzie always worried about ranking in the top three when the deep questions were asked. To stutter under the bright headlights, answer incorrectly, or misunderstand the question entirely could be detrimental for a beauty queen's career. Swallowing her fears, she took a deep breath.

In ten minutes Kenzie was scheduled to give her point of view and concerns for the three buildings up for sale—one of them being the one Ramon was interested in. Kenzie would be fair if given the chance to speak about which business proposal best suited Southwood history. Erin, still interested in the post office building as well, wanted to build a clinic. While Kenzie thought a clinic would be perfect, the fact that there was a veterinarian's office right around the corner from the building seemed weird to her. Besides, Kenzie doubted Erin wanted to settle down in Southwood. She was just doing this to get under Kenzie's skin.

"I hope I'm not interrupting," said a familiar feminine voice at the door.

Kenzie glanced up and felt her cheeks move as she smiled at the sight of her mother. "Mom!"

Paula Hairston-Swayne always managed to look as if she'd stepped off the pages of a fashion magazine. Her kelly green top matched her eyes. Her red hair defied the humidity and hung straight down her back and over her shoulder, ending in a perfect single curl. "Good. I thought you weren't speaking to me for a while there."

Kenzie moved around her desk, inwardly cursing at the future bruise that would form where her hip hit its sharp corner. Her hip then brushed against the boxes Ramon had sent over, the ones they'd found in the basement a few weeks ago. She wondered if he'd made any leeway with the washed-out ballots they'd found. A rigged election? A teacher's popular test passed down from year to year? Kenzie made a mental note to come back upstairs after the meeting to bring them back to the apartment for the rest of her time off. She'd promised Margaret she'd stay away.

"Why wouldn't I speak to you?"

"You've been so busy with this new man," Paula said. "I've seen the two of you around town looking all cozy. You and your beau have been so into each other, whether it was at Lexi's studio or the park for lunch. I even called your cell and your house line, and both went to voice mail."

Mother and daughter united in a hug. A twinge of guilt struck Kenzie. How could she begin to explain that what had started off as a front was turning into something more? Ending the hug, Paula placed her hand at Kenzie's temple, by her tucked-back hair. "No product, dear?"

"It's June, Mom," Kenzie said drily and prayed her mom dropped this smothering conversation.

Paula pointed to her perfectly coiffed hair. Besides when she was poolside, Kenzie never saw her mother's red hair out of place.

"Tell me you're going to recommend your cousin's clinic."

"Way to get right to the point, Mommy," Kenzie said, folding her arms under her breasts. Why did she feel like a middle-schooler about to be lectured by the principal?

"Sorry, but I know you're going to speak to the council in a few minutes and I just wanted to plead with you."

Kenzie sighed. "Why is it so important for you to have Erin here?"

Jealousy reared its ugly head. Erin was already Auntie Bren's favorite. Kenzie got that Erin was her mother's niece but did Paula always have to put her needs above her daughter's?

"I think it would do Erin some good if she moved back here for a while."

"Starting a clinic is going to take more than a while," Kenzie reminded her mother. "It's a big commitment and I've already told her starting it downtown is not historically sound. Dr. Fredd's office opened in 1870 just outside of downtown because people paid him in livestock."

"Fast-forward a hundred and fifty years later, Kenzie," her mother said while pinching the bridge of her nose, "and people now use money for currency." Paula paused, clamping her red-stained lips together. "What do you have against your cousin?"

"Where do I begin?"

"Kenzie, Erin's sisters are both married now."

While Paula ticked off the reasons why Kenzie needed to lighten up on her cousin, Kenzie half listened. Kenzie didn't bother bringing up the fact she and Erin were the same age. Why did Erin get empathy?

"And with the business taking off," Paula continued, "she's really just going through the motions at work."

"When do the two of you even talk?"

"We talk," said Paula, "Just as you and your Aunt Jody do."

Avoiding her mother's glare, Kenzie sighed and walked toward the window, her mother hot on her heels. She had spoken with Aunt Jody just this morning to confirm she was attending the sesquicentennial.

"I know you two still talk, even though after thirty years, she still won't speak to me because she believes I stole the crown out from under her."

"C'mon. Mom, you know the title meant a lot more to Aunt Jody than it did to you."

Paula folded her arms across her chest. The bow of the green silk blouse she wore crumpled. "I cannot have this conversation with you, Mackenzie."

"Because I'm a Swayne?" Kenzie cocked her head to the side. "I'm still half Hairston."

Paula snorted. "Your biggest claim to fame is being the last Swayne to win the title."

Actually her biggest claim to fame was earning her PhD, but Kenzie didn't bother clarifying. "Well, Mother," Kenzie said in clipped tones, "I need to hurry and go meet with the committee so I can get home and polish my tiara."

"Be serious."

"I am." The five-o'clock bell went off in the tower. "Look, I don't have time to sit here and discuss my issues with Erin, but you should know me well enough to know that I wouldn't hold my history with her against her in business." When her mother still didn't smile or look relieved, Kenzie huffed. "Besides, I am not the sole person deciding which business will open. I am just giving my professional opinion about the makeup and history of Southwood."

Her lips slightly moving in a frown, Paula glanced over her daughter. "I suppose."

"Thank you, Mother."

"Can we talk about your hair?"

"It's the middle of June," Kenzie said, stepping toward the stairwell. She needed to leave. "There is absolutely no reason for me to put anything in my hair right now."

"There's always a reason, dear," Paula called out to her daughter as the heavy doors closed and echoed down the stairs.

The Economic Development Council was made up of members of the city council and other local representatives, such as the mayor and his friends. Kenzie made an inner eye roll at having to face a few of these gentlemen. As town historian, Kenzie's opinion mattered if Southwood wanted to maintain its historic integrity. The mayor and his pals wanted to generate revenue, which she understood but in order to remain true to Southwood being a small town and priding itself on that, they did not need to bring in franchises. Her purpose today was to prove the town could still survive on local business. People drove from all over for the experience.

"The committee will now recognize Mackenzie Swayne, Southwood historian. Dr. Swayne, do you have anything to add concerning the list of buildings up for restoration?"

Pushing away from the mahogany rolling chair, Kenzie approached the wooden podium. The seersucker suit clung to her elbows, restricting movement as she shuffled her papers.

"Thank you, Miss Leena," said Kenzie, trying not to smile at her friend. When not working on the volunteer committee, Miss Leena manned the administrative desk at Southwood High School and often she was the one making the call for substitute teachers. Kenzie always accepted.

"I'd like the records to reflect the buildings up for sale."

Alexander leaned forward and cleared his throat into the silver microphone in front of him. "Let the records show that this will be Miss Swayne's recommendation."

"Dr. Swayne," Miss Leena corrected.

"I stand corrected," Alexander said with a head nod. "We're just trying to make the committee aware that what *Dr.* Swayne recommends is simply that, a recommendation. I have been hired to ensure Southwood's growth by bringing in new businesses, whether or not the buildings housing them are old."

"Historic." Kenzie savored being able to correct Alexander. "The buildings are historic. And our charming history is what brings visitors to our town. If we want to keep our revenue flowing, we need to preserve not just our physical buildings but also monitor what we put in these buildings." Kenzie took a sip of water from the clear glass on the podium. Out of the corner of her eye she spied Ramon in a light blue oxford, one leg crossed over his other and his hair secured back. She cleared her throat and tried to stay focused.

"Of course, with technology today," she continued, "we can't honestly expect to bring old jobs back like the film store, but we can pay homage to the business with a museum shop. We were already given a lot of historic donations last Christmas when we had our parade. We have clothes and paintings and old pictures to put in a museum if one were built."

"There are several buildings," said another councilman. "Which of those do you suggest the museum be placed?"

"I think the old post office would be perfect. There are several floors to fill. Plus it is smack downtown. I understand Mr. Reyes is interested in the building and we've discussed at length the need for such a facility for the community." Kenzie's heart raced with excitement. The council, Alexander not included, all nodded their heads with approval. Out the corner of her eye Kenzie saw Erin shake her head. Even though her mother wasn't in the room, Kenzie knew her mother was here in spirit...just with Erin. The kelly green dress Erin wore screamed of Paula's influence. She pushed their disapproving frowns out of her mind.

"With all due respect to the people wanting to bring in a commercial business, we don't need a private clinic. Southwood, Black Wolf Creek, Peachville and Samaritan have been thriving with the Four Points General. We don't need private practices. Four Points General has united the four cities since the First World War, and as for a sports bar, we have Shenanigans."

"Shenanigans is a place children can visit," interrupted Mayor Anson.

Kenzie took a deep breath and willed herself not to roll

her eyes. She hated the mayor. Not because he'd hired his best friend, Alexander, but because the man was an obsessive creep. Last year he became obsessed with her fellow beauty queen, Waverly Crowne. His obsession had almost cost Waverly into losing her chance to run for Miss Georgia and he thought he'd gotten away with it. Well, not if Kenzie had anything to do with it. This fall she planned on backing his opponent, whomever that might be.

"There are other sports bars around town, Mayor," Kenzie said, reminding the committee. "They're just not downtown in the founding square. Mr. Mayor, I assure you I am not here to exact some form of moral judgment. I simply was asked my opinion as a historian what was needed and if any of these proposals for the structures work with what's in the history books."

"And you're not a fan of a sports bar, which will bring in revenue?" Anson asked.

I'm not a fan of you, she thought. "As I've stated, this is my opinion."

"And there's a bid for a clinic downtown," said another councilman. The man was elderly and placed his thick black-rimmed glasses on his face. "Or is it a rehab?"

Erin tiptoed to the microphone on her side of the room. "A rehab center, Mr. Silas."

"And you are?"

"Erin," Erin replied with her hands clasped behind her back. "Erin Hairston."

"And you, Miss Historian, do you think a clinic fits the historic entity of Southwood?"

Those on the panel, aware of Erin and Kenzie's relations, leaned forward. Erin stood by her podium and faced Kenzie with her hand on her hip. Kenzie shrugged and leaned close to the microphone.

"No, I don't."

The shocked gasps almost deafened Kenzie. She gave her last recommendation and sat back down in her seat. Blood pounded between her ears. For the rest of the meeting she couldn't do anything but stare straight ahead, well aware of the daggers Erin shot her. When the dismissal gavel fell, Kenzie leaped from her seat in order to catch up with Erin, who stormed out as soon as possible.

Kenzie caught up with her cousin just outside the doors of the meeting room. Late evening sun spilled into the foyer. "Erin, I wanted to talk to you for a moment." Kenzie stepped in her cousin's way before she left the building. Like Kenzie's, Erin's complexion didn't help her hide her emotions.

Stone-faced, Erin turned to glare at her cousin. "What?"

"I don't want you to walk away mad and think I was being mean."

Erin dramatically leaned backward. "You?" she gestured toward Kenzie. "You be mean? Never."

The committee members leaving watched the interaction. Kenzie leaned in close. "Can we go somewhere and talk?"

"Oh, so you don't get embarrassed in front of your co-workers like you just did to me in front of the whole town?"

"Erin, I tried to tell you before I didn't think a clinic downtown was a good idea," Kenzie explained. "I also spoke with Stephen Reyes, who has several places he thought would be perfect, especially a little bit on the out-skirts of town, just like Dr. Fredd's."

Erin rolled her eyes. "You just love leaving me out of things."

Ramon stepped out of the double doors, shaking hands with the mayor. His eyes narrowed on Kenzie, then his brows rose with curiosity.

"I'm not leaving you out of anything, Erin. I was asked my opinion about the history of Southwood and I gave it."

Erin smirked and glanced over her shoulder. "And you think a non-profit was a part of the history of Southwood? Let's be honest. We both know why you're doing it. You're so hard up for a man you'll sell your own family out."

Kenzie gasped. "Talk about selling family out—do you not recall a time when you openly campaigned against me?"

"For Miss Southwood?" Erin leaned backward, swaying her hips in dramatic fashion, clearly a habit she learned from Paula. "I was trying to save you."

"Save me?" Kenzie realized her voice had gone up an octave when the people in the hall stopped walking. Ramon came to her side, tugging her elbow.

"Let's get out of here, Kenzie."

"In a minute." Kenzie pulled her arm away. "Save me how, Erin?"

Erin placed her hands on her hips. "You were always more than a beauty queen, Kenzie. I always worried you winning would change you, but I guess deep down inside you are a vapid airhead who is so afraid to attend a public event without a date you had to go and hire someone."

"I—"

Erin silenced her with a wave of her hand. "Save it. He didn't want you a year ago. Clearly your embarrassed, desperate ass still hasn't learned your lesson. He's only using you to get your approval for the building. The building you could have saved for your flesh and blood."

Chapter 9

Once away from the courthouse and just outside of the city limits, Kenzie and Ramon arrived at Magnolia Palace. Cars, vans and SUVs filled the paved parking lot off to the side of the building. A puff of smoke billowed in the sky from the backyard. With it being Thursday evening, Kenzie figured Jessilyn was prepping for the barbecue on Saturday that she'd wanted to bring into town. The young chef's dish smelled like it would be worth eating and getting homemade barbecue sauce all over her suit.

Given what Erin said, doubt crept into Kenzie's mind. Being here on the grounds of Magnolia Palace, alone with Ramon, brought back the memories of their parting. *He's only using you.* Erin's words repeated in her mind. When Ramon led Kenzie on the path on the outskirts of the hotel, Kenzie questioned him. "I have on heels and you're taking me into the woods?"

"I can throw you over my shoulder if you like," Ramon teased.

Tempting offer, but Kenzie digressed and followed him over the pier to a private path she'd never remembered seeing before when she'd been here. Pine needles blanketed the forest floor. Crickets and katydids played a symphony for them as the sun slowly began to sink over the treetops. Any ounce of irritation over Erin's harsh words dissipated at the sight in the clearing of the magnolia trees. White magnolia petals circled a blue-and-white gingham blanket. On top of the blanket sat a brown wicker basket with a loaf of French bread hanging out of one side and a bottle of champagne from the other. Fresh fruit and cheese sat on a white plate with blue trim.

"When did you have time to set this up?" Kenzie asked, turning toward Ramon. He stood behind her, leaning against a tree.

The sleeves of his light blue shirt were rolled to his elbows. Her heart stopped. "Can't I do something nice for my lady?"

Ramon motioned for Kenzie to sit. She kicked off her heels before stepping onto the blanket. He followed suit and helped ease her down onto the blanket. Ramon grabbed the bottle of champagne and opened it. The cork flew off into the leaves. "Now, that's how you end a day like today."

"Should I be afraid to drink this?" Kenzie asked, lifting a flute of champagne in toast.

Ramon raised his glass for a toast. "Why would I want to poison you?"

"Because of my belief in a not-for-profit business in town, something for the kids. If you were still planning on starting up a business franchise, I may have influenced the committee to turn you down." Kenzie chewed her bottom lip and recalled Erin's words. Ramon didn't want her last year. Why would he want her now?

With a half shrug, Ramon shook his head. "We aren't together because of what you can do for me, Kenzie. Let's get that understood." He clinked his glass against hers. A dove in the tree flew away into the blue sky.

"Together?" Kenzie repeated with a smile. "I think it's time we have a talk about that."

"Uh-oh." Ramon set his glass down on the blanket they sat on. "This doesn't sound good. We've got two more events to go to."

"No," Kenzie said with a raised brow. "I never said yes to the previous weddings. You showed up uninvited to the first one and the second one you came to because Auntie Bren invited you."

"In retrospect, don't you find it weird your aunt would invite me to someone else's wedding?"

"You've met her—does anything she says surprise you?"

"No, I guess not."

"Exactly," Kenzie replied smugly.

Ramon leaned back on his elbow. His long legs, encased in a pair of medium-washed denim jeans, stretched over the blanket. "Well, what is it you want to say about your events? Are we not attending the gala together?"

Kenzie raised her index finger. "Let's keep in mind that I never said yes and now that we're done with the committee, I think we should wait."

Ramon sat up. "Wait for what?"

Kenzie set her glass down. "Hear me out first."

"Are you ending things?"

"Have we started things?" Kenzie asked. "If you weren't interested in the building, would we still be here?"

Ramon reached out and took her hand. She loved the security she felt at the touch.

"Kenzie, I broke my No Kenzie rule for you."

"What?"

"I vowed after your recent antics to stay away from you so you wouldn't torment me around town."

Playfully Kenzie squeezed Ramon's hand, for whatever

good that did—his hands were too big for hers to cause him any pain. "Stop playing."

Ramon wedged his hand between her thighs. "But I like playing with you."

A deep inhale didn't stop the chills of desire creeping down her back. "I just want to say I don't need you to escort me to the gala. You don't have to show up for whatever odd reason you've been using."

"'Odd reason'?" Ramon squeezed the thickness of her inner thigh. "I can think of several reasons. Are you saying you don't like when I come over?"

"I didn't say that." Kenzie shivered. "I'm just... I don't..." Her words were lost as Ramon's hand crawled up her legs. His mouth found her neck. "Ramon, I need you to understand that this is confusing and we're getting everyone involved."

"All right," said Ramon, sitting next to her. "Everyone involved how?"

"Everyone believes we're a couple."

"Aren't we? I called you my lady."

Kenzie shrugged her shoulders.

"If you never said yes to my proposal, then what's transpired between us is something real, don't you think?" Ramon bumped his shoulder against hers. "Which is it?"

"But the committee today..."

"We're celebrating right now, Kenzie," said Ramon. "While you and Erin were talking, I got the bid. I start construction on the building next week. The committee wanted your opinion but they valued my dollar amount."

"Please don't tell me you agreed to put in a bar." She scanned Ramon's face for an answer but got none.

"I haven't agreed to anything but the purchase. But if it worries you so much, what if I promise you I won't put a sports bar in the building?"

In truth, Ramon could do whatever he wanted. If the committee had wanted to accept the bid from Erin, they could have. Kenzie pressed her lips together. "I'm trusting you."

"I'm not going to let you down," Ramon whispered. "I don't see how being separated from you is a solution. Because of what your cousin said? Baby, she was mad."

If Erin was mad, she knew the exact low blow to hit Kenzie with. Even her mother had taken Erin's side. Toppled with the realization the committee had truly only wanted her opinion, Kenzie couldn't help but feel utterly useless. "Well, she called me out on my BS, Ramon. I did need someone to take me to the weddings. I was embarrassed to have everyone see me arrive dateless without any prospects."

"Erin attended solo, as well," Ramon pointed out.

Another shrug; Kenzie still didn't feel better. "I guess," she mumbled. "I still would rather make sure we're not together-together at the gala. Will that hurt your feelings?"

"Hell yeah," said Ramon, flopping onto this backside.

The move was so childish, Kenzie giggled. She leaned over his frame. "Can you do that again for me, but this time will you flail your legs in the air?"

"Are you mocking my pain?"

"Pain?"

"You're telling me I can't see you."

"That's not what I said. You're free to attend the gala, just on your own. You're free to attend the pageant, just on your own."

"That leaves one last wedding."

The wind blew, showering them with a sweet magnolia scent. Kenzie closed her eyes and enjoyed the moment. She splayed her hand against his chest, over his beating heart. When she opened her eyes she found Ramon staring at her.

"Jesus, you're so beautiful," Ramon whispered. His hand snaked out and cupped her behind her neck, bringing her head close to his.

Kenzie tucked a stray hair behind her ear. She pressed a sweet kiss against his lips. "Does this mean you're not mad anymore?"

"Oh, I'm pretty mad." Ramon tucked his hand behind his head and turned his gaze. "I have to start obeying my No Kenzie rule again."

"Stop saying that." Kenzie dug her nails into his chest. Ramon playfully continued to ignore her, staring aimlessly into the sky.

"I don't hear anything."

Shifting from kneeling beside him, Kenzie straddled his waist. "You can't hear me, huh? Can you feel me?"

In order to continue his charade, Ramon sighed deeply and closed his eyes.

"Oh well, if you can't feel me, I guess you can't feel this." She lowered her head and kissed his neck. His Adam's apple rose and his gulp echoed. As Kenzie lowered her mouth from his neck, her hands unbuttoned his shirt and slid beneath his cotton undershirt. She loved the feel of his hard muscles underneath his silky skin.

The button of his slacks slipped out of its hole with ease and his zipper coasted downward. A hard erection pressed against the blue boxer shorts underneath and Kenzie was obliged to help free it from its constraints.

Ramon moved to his elbows. "What are you…?"

"Shh." She blew against the tip of his shaft. "You don't hear me, you don't feel me, remember?" Kenzie teased him with a lick before taking him in her mouth. The ground shook when Ramon flopped onto his back. Kenzie smiled to herself, knowing good and well she had his undivided attention. But she was suddenly distracted by the sound of voices.

Stopping, Kenzie came to her knees. "Did you hear that?"

"What?" Ramon asked breathlessly. "No, nothing, don't stop now."

"I'm serious, Ramon."

They were in a secluded area on Ramon's property. They'd taken the path to a private spot. Only Jessilyn was supposed to know where to set up the picnic, and she wasn't coming back here.

"Ramon?" a voice called out to them, a woman's voice.

Kenzie narrowed her eyes on Ramon. Clearly he heard it too and sat up. "That can't be."

"Who is it?" Kenzie asked.

"I think it's my mother."

"You, are you back here?" a deep man's voice asked.

"And my brother Julio," Ramon added. He jumped to his feet, pulling Kenzie with him and adjusted himself. "Cool, you get to meet the family tonight."

"What?" Kenzie exclaimed. "I'm not about to meet your mother when two seconds ago..." She stopped what she was saying and touched her bottom lip.

"You're cute." Ramon laughed, bringing his lips down to hers. "C'mon."

"No, I'm serious. Go cut them off before they discover us and I die of embarrassment."

Ramon sighed heavily. "Only because I don't want you to die before finishing what we're starting."

Kenzie popped him on the arm and turned him around. "Go."

"Okay, fine, twisted woman."

"I'll wait here and meet your parents tomorrow."

* * *

The sesquicentennial celebration turned out to be everything Kenzie said it would be. Residents of Southwood came out in droves for the afternoon picnic and tour through the town. People traveled from as far as North Carolina and south Florida to participate in the activities. Children's activities ranged from sack races to doll- and dressmaking outside Grits and Glam Gowns. Tables were set up for pick-up sticks, a game introduced to Southwood.

The high school's baseball team was scheduled to play an afternoon game against two dozen men. Kenzie suggested anyone who wanted to play against the district champions were allowed to form one team. The list grew to over thirty. Ramon hit one homer, but it didn't make a difference and the newcomers were annihilated by teenaged boys. Kenzie summed up the mercy game with a history lesson. Baseball was introduced to Southwood when a Union soldier from the New York area decided to stay in the cozy town.

The activities for the day kept Kenzie busy and Ramon occupied with his family. She enjoyed hearing the origins of the town and how the family had created their dynasty. It reminded her of her own, without the backstabbing cousins. They knew everything about Villa San Juan, stories were passed on from generation to generation. Kenzie had arranged for horse-drawn carriage rides for the elders over sixty. People were also able to ride in vintage cars courtesy of Crowne Restoration, an automobile shop specializing in classic cars. Vendors set up shop outside of the businesses on the sidewalks and some set up carts and tables in the grassy square in front of City Hall. Business owners dropped their prices for one day and former high school bands from graduating classes of each decade gave an ensemble at the amphitheater.

* * *

As the sun set, free concerts ran downtown but for those who wanted to spend the money to join the black tie gala at the Southwood Country Club. Ramon started the evening off seated at a round table fit for twelve people. His mother and father, Ana and Julio Senior, were across from him. Next to his mother was Kimber, then Lexi and Stephen. Raul, the second-youngest brother, sat next to Ramon, and on the other side of Ramon was his oldest brother, Julio Junior, then Nate and his lovely wife, Amelia, who had a film crew documenting tonight's celebration. Beside Amelia sat Carlos and his wife, celebrity chef Grace Colon.

"Julio," Ramon said, turning to his right. "What did you think of today's events?"

"Spectacular," said Julio. The eldest of the Torres brothers looked tall even when seated. Julio was what Ramon considered a pretty boy and a snob. Women flocked to him. *His personality could be better*, Ramon thought inwardly, but overall, he had to hand it to his brother for trying to be the best he could be.

"I think we need something like this," said Raul, a year older than Ramon and a successful nightclub owner in Villa San Juan. Of course his club was attached to what was probably the most successful restaurant in town in the state of Florida, so Ramon might be biased there.

"There's that lovely Kenzie Swayne," Ana said and gawked, clasping her hands over her heart. "Do you realize she put this whole thing together? We could use her organizational skills at this year's Crystal Coqui. She truly understands the importance of honoring family tradition. I had the good fortune to speak with her this afternoon. She was so kind as to give me a history lesson about Southwood and so generous to tell me more about the surrounding cities."

As Ana held court about her encounter with Kenzie this afternoon, Ramon thought about his night with the belle of the ball. He glanced across the table where his beaming mother looked and spotted Kenzie immediately. It was hard not to miss her. To help get into the authenticity of the time when Southwood was established, she wore an old-fashioned patchwork hoop skirt, bonnet and shawl. Only Kenzie could make the dress sexy.

"Oh yeah," Nate chimed in, snapping his fingers. "It was her family Ramon stole his hotel from."

That's the last time you'll come over and work out, Ramon thought, narrowing his eyes on his cousin.

"¿*Qué*, Ramon?" Ana gasped, clutching the diamond-and-sapphire necklace designed by Kane Diamonds as a fortieth wedding anniversary present. For generations the Torres men showered their women with diamonds. Ramon wondered if it was too soon to buy Kenzie a congratulatory tennis bracelet for doing such a wonderful job today.

As Nate smirked across the table, Ramon's hand wrapped around his glass tumbler of rum. Better the beverage than his cousin's throat. Ana blinked her large eyes in his direction. If there ever was a person Ramon did not want to disappoint, it was his mother. He'd been her baby boy. Growing up and watching his brothers make their mistakes, Ramon learned how to stay on her good side. Some sweet treat—either coconut *tembleque*, a slice of custardy flan, or flakey, cream cheese and guava pastries—*quesitos de guayaba*—was always his reward for good behavior. There were the special times his mother slipped him a couple of *polvorones* cookies for letting her know what his brothers were up to. Ramon blamed his childhood obesity on his tattling. But the melt-in-your-mouth shortbread cookies were divine. "I didn't steal anything. No one lived in the place for over fifty years. I made an investment. I've already spoken to the family and everyone wishes me success."

"Except Kenzie," muttered Nate. Because his cousins had grown up with him like brothers, Ramon's cousins had been collateral damage when it came to Ramon tattling and getting his sweet treats from his mother. So Ramon guessed this playful underhandedness was payback. Just as Nate reached for a piece of red pepper off the crudité plate, his wife, Amelia, must have kicked him under the table. "Ouch."

Thanks, Ramon mouthed to Amelia.

"His investment paid off, Tía Ana," said Stephen. "The Magnolia Palace is the most successful hotel in town."

"And that's with the Brutti Hotel," added Lexi.

"You know, I spoke to Gianni a few weeks ago," said Raul. "He wants to add a nightclub to one of his chains in Miami."

"You'd be perfect to consult," Ramon's mother boasted. "We'll have to stop by and see him while we're in town."

Ramon had put his parents up at Magnolia Palace for the weekend. They'd arrived in typical fashion, loud and carrying food. Jessilyn was a bit overwhelmed when his mother took over the kitchen but like a true chef, she sat back and took notes. It didn't hurt that one of the best chefs in Florida was in his kitchen, as well. Grace was a welcome addition to the Torres family. She was the first to get one of Ana and Julio's boys to the altar.

For some odd reason the idea of marriage made Ramon turn and locate Kenzie. He sat back in his chair and watched Kenzie make her way toward him with a wide smile across her face. His heart swelled and now that he was used to the feeling, he liked it.

"Look at you smiling," Nate said, gaining Ramon's attention again. "Ouch," he added quickly and turned his head toward Amelia. "Why do you keep hitting me?"

"Because you are trying to embarrass your cousin and now is not the time. Behave."

Kimber, seated next to Amelia, snickered. "Don't be too hard on him, Aunt Amelia."

"What?" Stephen and Nate chorused and turned their ears toward the college student.

The matriarch at the table dropped her fork and glared at Nate and Stephen for Kimber's use of the word "aunt." When Kimber's father had passed away, it was discovered she'd never been forced to learn Spanish growing up. It had become a longstanding joke about Kimber and Philly not being able to speak Spanish. Smiling, Grace lifted her goblet of water and coughed. Everyone else caught on. A few years ago, Grace too couldn't speak a word of Spanish. She understood.

When she realized her faux pas, Kimber rolled her hazel eyes toward the chandelier. "*Tía*," she corrected. Everyone at the table laughed. "You all realize I am almost twenty-one and a double major in college, right?" Kimber asked. No one responded. "Ugh. Anyway, *Tía* Amelia, I think it's great to see Ramon all flustered. It serves him right."

"Serves me right?" Ramon blurted.

"Yes." Kimber cut her eyes to him and then back to Amelia. "He's broken many hearts around town."

"What broken hearts?" Ramon asked. "And why am I bothering to ask a kid?"

"*Mijo*, are you meeting girls here?" asked his mother. "Because it is about time you settle down."

"Leave the boy alone," mumbled his father as he pressed his fork through a lemon cupcake, courtesy of The Cupcakery. Most of Ramon's life, Julio Senior had never said much. He went to work at Torres Towers, helped maintain the family name and business and came home. He expected dinner on the table by six and only disciplined when his wife told him it needed to be done. He was a man of few words. Ana clamped her mouth closed.

"Julio and Raul haven't settled down," Ramon pointed out. "Why aren't we having this discussion with them?"

Ana fingered a diamond on her necklace. "All of you need to settle down. I'm not getting any younger and my baby sister already has a grandchild in college."

"*Gracias*, Tía Ana." Kimber beamed. "I didn't mean to say Ramon has been like Tío Nate." Kimber nodded in Amelia's direction. "No offense, Amelia."

"None taken," Amelia said with a light laugh.

"Ramon's been so caught up with work that he never takes time for himself."

The men all frowned. Ramon chuckled to himself. This must be what Kenzie endured with her family. Speaking of which, he noticed she was caught up talking to Mr. Myers, the retired history teacher. Ramon liked the old man but knew talking to him took at least an hour. Ramon was ready to reclaim Kenzie.

"Excuse me, Ma," Ramon said, pushing away from the table.

"Where's he going?" asked Julio.

"To get his beauty queen," Ramon heard Lexi say as he walked away.

At five hundred a plate, the crowd tonight was exclusive, yet the room was still packed. Ramon made his way through the crowd, bumping shoulders with some of the town's prominent members. Kenzie had sat on the decorating committee and brought in the photographs they'd found in the basement of the old post office. People studied the old paperwork and tried to guess whether the bizarre signatures belonged to their family members.

"There you are."

Ramon blew out an annoyed sigh when Alexander stepped in front of him, a dangerous space to put himself in, especially when it stopped him from getting to Kenzie.

"What do you want?"

"Whoa," Alexander said, holding his hands up in the air. "I come in peace."

"I'm not sure what *peace* means to you."

"The word may be lost on you." Alexander smoothed down the front of his white tuxedo shirt. "The last time we came across each other, you sucker punched me."

"You were drunk and advancing on Kenzie with her back turned," Ramon reminded him.

"Kenzie and I go way back," said Alexander.

"Yes, she told me how the two of you were engaged at one point in time," Ramon went on, eager to wipe the smirk off Alexander's face. "And she told me about how you cheated on her." The smirk dropped and Alexander scratched the back of his head. "Yeah, so before you get inebriated tonight, let me warn you—quit while you're ahead."

"Now see," Alexander said, collecting his thoughts, "I came here to discuss the matter of the ballots you brought to my office a few weeks ago to have analyzed."

"I didn't give you anything."

"I understand, but the cute little receptionist downstairs handed me the results."

Ramon studied the man. Clearly the ballots were important to him. "I'm sure somewhere in there is an illegal offense. I'll have my lawyer look into it. But for now, if you'll excuse me…"

"Don't you want to look at them?"

"You would like that, wouldn't you?" Ramon asked.

Alexander shook his head left and right. "I already

know what the contents are, considering I'm the right hand of the mayor."

"So save the two of us the drama and tell me what it is you found out." Ramon tucked the envelope into his jacket.

"The results aren't from an election ballot. Something a little closer to home. Want to guess?"

Ramon stepped forward to leave. He needed to find Kenzie. "I don't have time for games."

Alexander stepped in Ramon's way. "Before you head off to Kenzie, let me warn you, the contents of the envelope concern her."

Gritting his back teeth, Ramon willed himself not to slug him.

Alexander took his moment to continue. "The ballots you found belonged to the Miss Southwood Pageant from ten years ago. Turns out all these ballots belong to my sister, Felicia Ward," said Alexander. "Well, Crawford now. But I digress. I wonder what will happen when this comes to light."

If this came to light, Kenzie would be humiliated. He knew how important it was for Kenzie to be the last Miss Southwood. If she had not won fair and square, this would devastate her and it would kill him to see her so upset. Ramon vowed to never let that happen to her.

"I mean, everyone knows Kenzie as the last Swayne to win a crown, allegedly."

"You'll be wise to keep this to yourself, Alexander."

"Relax," said Alexander. "Kenzie's been through a lot in her life and I don't want to cause her any more pain and embarrassment. I only wanted to tell you ahead of time because I know how nuts Kenzie is about history stuff and I didn't want her to find out this way. There were only twenty-five votes for my sister stashed away. I understand the voting was done by ballots, so there's no telling just how many people voted."

Not like he'd been to many but the last time Ramon had attended a beauty pageant, there'd been a panel of judges. Ramon didn't believe a word Alexander said but right now, it was all the information he had.

"I see you're going to mull it over," Alexander observed. "Like I said, I didn't want Kenzie to be caught off guard looking these over. I'll let you do whatever you want with them." Alexander nodded his head and passed by Ramon.

Ramon turned, still in disbelief about the results and uncertain who knew about them. If anyone got wind of a rigged pageant, Kenzie would surely lose her title. She had her degree and she was proud of it. But knowing she was a fraudulent beauty queen would sting. There'd be no coming back from the humiliation. He wasn't going to let this mar their evening. Ramon turned and watched Alexander grab Mayor Anson by the elbow and head over to the Torres family. Julio rose and shook hands. Ramon felt a tug at his upper lip at the sight of the three of them. He imagined all the smarmy deals Alexander and Anson were trying to throw at his brother. Ramon didn't know how often the Economic Development Council met but he had a distinct feeling Julio might be attending the next meeting.

"There you are."

Ramon's heart lurched at the sound of Kenzie's Southern drawl. He turned toward her and stretched out his arms for her to step into his embrace. He plastered a smile on his face.

"Were you looking for me?" Ramon asked. "Because I was heading over to rescue you from Mr. Myer."

Kenzie cast a glance over her shoulder and then looked back at Ramon.

His heart swelled again. "Hello, beautiful."

Nodding her head, Kenzie blushed. "Thanks. I'm feeling pretty ridiculous in this getup."

"I think this might be the sexiest thing I've seen you in. Lexi did a great job."

"This is an authentic calico dress circa 1870, hand sewn by Elvira Pendergrass, a distant relative of Lexi's."

So dressmaking ran in the family, Ramon thought. He'd seen some of the racy designs Lexi came up with and gave a silent prayer of thanks for Elvira's common sense—she'd left the bodice modest. Considering Alexander was lurking around, Ramon didn't want too much of Kenzie showing. As a matter of fact, he was tempted to take off his jacket to cover her up. At least her legs were fully covered. They were his.

"I had the pleasure of meeting your mother earlier this afternoon." Kenzie looked over his shoulder and waved.

"She was just telling us." Ramon reached out snaked his arm around Kenzie's waist. "It's hard to impress her. How'd you do it?"

Kenzie's dark eyes widened. "Just your typical five-minute afternoon thunderstorm brought us together. I saw her walking by herself and pulled her into Osborne Books. We sat and had tea with Miss Gwen."

The only reason Ramon knew Miss Gwen was because Kenzie insisted they visit her and the bookstore to get more information about the photos of the old city. Kenzie amazed him. With everything going on today, she'd taken time out to have tea with a stranger. He inhaled deeply, his heart thumping against his chest. Ramon dipped his head toward hers, liking the way she bit her bottom lip and hesitated.

"Public affection?" Kenzie asked, looking around.

"You're damn straight." He brought his mouth down to hers.

Chapter 10

"It is about time you and Ramon figured things out."

A short while later Kenzie found herself cornered in the ladies' room by Maggie. Kenzie ran the curve of her summer-strawberry-red lipstick over her bottom lip, which was becoming her favorite product from Ravens Cosmetics. Every time she wore it she ended out in some form of make-out session with Ramon. Her pulse raced with excitement. She needed to hurry and get back out there to him.

"What are you talking about?" Kenzie asked her sister.

"Don't act like you're reapplying your lipstick because you left it all on your wineglass," Maggie teased. "We both know you and Ramon have been sneaking off kissing."

"Well, he has been trying to help keep Auntie Bren off my back." Even as she said the words, she didn't believe them.

Judging from the scowl on Maggie's face, neither did her sister. "Sure, say whatever you want to fool yourself. I'm not going to argue with you."

"Thank you."

"On another note, good job on getting Aunt Jody into town."

Kenzie cleaned up any stray lipstick in the margins of her lips.

"I know, right? I am amazing," Kenzie boasted playfully.

Maggie rolled her eyes. "Whatever."

"Seriously, though." Kenzie sobered. "I was shocked she came. I pulled the great-niece card."

"Bailey," Maggie said with a thoughtful sigh.

"Who can resist?"

Kenzie turned and rested her hip against the white-and-gray marble countertop of the bathroom. "She certainly can't resist seeing another Swayne win another crown."

"Are you ready to give up your reign as the last Swayne to win?"

Kenzie shook her head from side to side. "It is going to be an honor to crown Bailey myself."

Maggie turned too, folding her arms across her gingham period dress. With her hair tied in two pigtails, Maggie reminded Kenzie of a stand-in for Dorothy in *The Wizard of Oz*.

"And soon Bailey will be crowning a new little baby Torres." In an attempt to be funny, Maggie reached over to rub her sister's stomach.

Kenzie slapped her hand away. "Cut that out."

"Don't want me to hurt the baby?" Maggie continued to tease.

Kenzie rolled her eyes.

"See, this is the point where you'd stop me and tell me nothing has happened between you and Ramon and that there's no way you could even remotely be pregnant."

"There is no way I can be pregnant, Maggie," Kenzie said with a straight face. She didn't want to discuss her intimate moments with Ramon with anyone else. Last summer Maggie knew too much. Plus, this way, if things didn't work out between her and Ramon, she wouldn't be embarrassed in front of anyone. Sure, last summer, Kenzie should have picked up on his noncommittal attitude. Things were different now. She felt in her heart things had changed.

"You keep kissing him."

"There's no harm in kissing." Kenzie twisted the gold tube of lipstick in her hands.

Someone flushed one of the stalls and the door opened up. Kenzie and Maggie shared a look, their eyes wide at the sight of Auntie Bren waltzing out toward the sink between them. Auntie Bren was dressed in a period piece like those all the founding members of Southwood had worn. She wore a high-necked, off-white gown with black buttons, very First World War.

"If you two think a woman gets pregnant by kissing," she began slowly in her haughty voice, "it's no wonder you're both still single."

Maggie cackled. "Auntie Bren, aren't you still single?"

Kenzie reached around her aunt and pinched Maggie's elbow. "Hush."

"I'm single by choice," Auntie Bren answered coolly. "Meanwhile, if you put down all of your electronic devices, both internet-ready and battery-included, you might find a man."

Maggie gaped. Kenzie tried not to laugh. No way had her eighty-five-year-old aunt just alluded to a vibrator.

"C'mon, Auntie," Kenzie said, trying to lighten the mood. "We saw you with Oscar Blakemore last week."

"That old guy?" Maggie reached in the breast lining of her bodice, took out her phone and flipped through it. "This guy?" She angled the phone for both of them to see a beautiful photo of Auntie Bren, in all her royal purple, and Oscar in an embrace.

The corners of Auntie Bren's lips turned up in a smile

but quickly turned down again. "That's the man I chose not to be with."

"I don't understand," said Maggie. "Is this the guy you wanted to make jealous with Ramon?"

"Mission accomplished," Kenzie said with a low whistle. "I thought he was going to knock Ramon out."

At the mention of the incident, Auntie Bren smiled softly. "I'm sorry to have placed him in jeopardy like that. He was such a good sport."

Maggie rested her hip on the porcelain counter. "Are you going to tell us who that man was to you?"

"That was a boyfriend of mine when I was fifteen."

"Fifteen?" Maggie and Kenzie chorused.

"What?" Auntie Bren asked innocently. "I wasn't always the matriarch of this family. I used to have a wild side."

"So what happened with you and Mr. Oscar?" Maggie asked.

Other women began trickling into the ladies' room in twos. Auntie Bren took Kenzie's lipstick and used it on herself. "Oscar went off to serve in World War II. When he returned three years later he was engaged to another woman."

"And you were heartbroken?" asked Maggie.

"Of course I was. I thought we were going to get married. I doubted myself because of him. I never learned to trust anyone."

Heartbroken, Kenzie shook her head and reached to hug her aunt. She hated the idea of her aunt being so devastated over one man that she closed her heart to future possibilities. It seemed so lonely. She had a brief taste of that loneliness last summer and compared to the closeness she felt with Ramon now, she never wanted to revisit that dark period in her life. "I'm so sorry. I didn't realize that."

"It's okay. I've chosen to be alone so I can concentrate on my girls," Auntie Bren said with a smile. "And can I say, dear," she said to Kenzie, "it's been a pleasure watching you and Ramon together these last few weeks. I can return to Miami knowing you're in good hands."

Ah, there was that, Kenzie thought. A shiver drove down her spine at the idea of Ramon's hands all over her. She wondered how long it was going to be before she got to spend the night with him again. With his parents and family in town she didn't expect him to leave them at the hotel, nor did she think he expected her to spend the night with him.

"Wait a minute." Maggie interrupted Kenzie's thoughts. "What is going to happen with you and Oscar? Is he going to move down to Miami, or will you move here?"

Kenzie shot her sister a glare. A month of Auntie Bren was enough.

"I mean, or will you guys move some place other than Southwood?" Maggie tried to recover but she sounded so awkward.

Auntie Bren handed Kenzie her lipstick back. "I am done with him."

"What?" The girls gaped.

"At eighty-seven years old he's still lying."

"About what?" they asked again in unison.

Auntie Bren rolled her eyes. "Grown folks' business," she said as if they weren't all adults here.

"What is it you kids say? Ain't nobody got time for that?"

Maggie choked on air.

Kenzie stepped backward. "Lord, let me get out of here."

"Well, wait," Auntie Bren said, taking hold of Kenzie's arm. "Have either of you seen Erin?"

Maggie shook her head from side to side. "Cousin Danielle told me Erin took off yesterday to meet a client, but wouldn't say who."

"You know she wants to open a clinic in town?" Auntie Bren asked Kenzie.

Kenzie shook her head and looked away, knowing what was coming next.

"What's wrong with Erin moving here and starting her business? Are you still mad at her for your beauty queen thing?"

"Nothing, I guess," Kenzie huffed and squared her shoulders. "Look, I tried to tell her I had another place in mind for her but she went off on me after the meeting the other night."

Auntie Bren tipped Kenzie's chin down. "She's family. Now, if you'll excuse me, I am going to mingle with my friends."

"By friends, do you mean Oscar?"

"By friends, do you mean your battery-operated ones?" Auntie Bren crassly responded as Maggie stood there with her mouth wide-open.

Kenzie linked her arm with her sister's. "Serves you right."

"Serves her right if I have a male stripper sent over to her nursing home in Miami."

"It's an assisted living facility," Kenzie corrected.

"Whatever. So you wouldn't care if she moved back here?"

"Not really."

"Because you're so preoccupied and in love with Ramon?" Maggie sung Ramon's name in a low, husky voice.

"Girl, let's go." Kenzie headed out the interior door of the women's bathroom. Maggie, still taunting her, mumbled and questioned if she needed to hurry up and leave so she could get back to Ramon. In truth, yes, Kenzie thought with a smile. Her heart fluttered against her rib cage. Of course she couldn't wait to stand next to Ramon's side.

These last few days with Ramon had been wonderful. After winning the bid for the post office, Ramon started working with his construction team. Top that off with his successful business at the Magnolia Palace, and Ramon was a busy man.

Eager, Kenzie pushed hard on the outer door and immediately hit someone.

"Jesus, girl," Aunt Jody snapped, shaking her hand. "Are you trying to kill me?"

Kenzie hugged her aunt. Even though it wasn't kosher to say, her father's sister was Kenzie's favorite relative. To Kenzie, Aunt Jody was always glamorous. She kept her chestnut-brown hair straight and in a trendy style like a bob, a flip, or even shaggy. Tonight Aunt Jody was participating in dressing up with the other founding family members. She didn't dress in the 1870s clothing. She chose the Roaring Twenties and was able to tuck her hair under and secure a white band around her head. She wore six strands of white pearls varying in size around her neck that hung down the front of her black flapper dress in a knot.

"Oh, dear child," Aunt Jody cooed, patting Kenzie's back. They were the same height. "I have missed you so much."

"What about me, Auntie Jody?" Maggie asked.

Aunt Jody scoffed in Kenzie's ear at the sound of *Auntie*. "Don't call me that. That's my aunt's deal. And Maggie, darling, how am I supposed to miss you when you're forever on the social media?"

"I get no love from this family," Maggie said with a

pout. "And to think, I have been off the grid since I've been here."

Aunt Jody moved to hug her other niece. "Your poor followers must be worried sick wondering where you are."

Kenzie hid her laugh by looking the other way. Aunt Jody grabbed her by the wrist and gave her a tug and held her back. "Where are you going?"

Kenzie shot Maggie a warning glare to keep quiet. It was one thing to have Auntie Bren or other people in her family think she was in a relationship until the month ended but she didn't want to lie to Aunt Jody. But would it really be a lie? Kenzie knew she was falling hard for Ramon. She just prayed he felt the same way. "I wanted to check on the guests."

"This isn't just *your* event," reminded Aunt Jody. "Let some of the other family members around town do some work. Where are the bastards? The Hairstons need to help."

Maggie giggled.

Kenzie made an apologetic smile toward the ladies walking up to the bathrooms. "Aunt Jody," she whispered close. After the overpowering scent of hairspray Kenzie got a whiff of gin. "Have you been drinking?"

Aunt Jody's dark eyes were red around the rims. "No wonder you have a doctorate."

Not everyone in the family spoke of Kenzie's education. She beamed but tried to remember now was not the time to brag. "Let's get you over to the table."

"I'll get some water," said Maggie, taking off.

Kenzie slipped Aunt Jody's arm over her shoulder and escorted her toward a private table away from the center of everything. They were close to the balcony door and Kenzie prayed the fresh air would do her aunt some good.

"You're such a dear," said Aunt Jody. "I was so afraid I messed things up for you."

"Messed what up, Aunt Jody?" asked Kenzie. She picked up a Martin Luther King fan with a Sinkford Funeral Home advertisement on the other side and began cooling off her aunt's face. Sweat beaded under the white band around her forehead but started to disappear with Kenzie's use of the fan.

Aunt Jody grabbed Kenzie by the wrist. "I fear you were involved with the beauty pageants because of the pressure I placed on you."

"Beauty pageants are in my blood, Aunt Jody," Kenzie assured her. "What's going on with you? Have you stayed away from Southwood all this time because of that?"

"Maybe."

"I entered Miss Southwood when I was eighteen hoping that I could get you to come back to town."

Aunt Jody scowled. "I told myself I'd never show my face around here after your father rigged my pageant so your mother could win."

Ah, the family skeletons.

"I'm sorry you think my mom stole the crown from you," said Kenzie, "but it's been over twenty years. Can we let it go? I mean, look at the first big step you've taken in such a time. You finally came back to Southwood after vowing to never step foot here again."

"Well, I've stepped foot." Aunt Jody giggled.

Kenzie narrowed her eyes. "What?"

"Never mind, sweetie. Where is that hunk you were kissing earlier?"

"You saw that?" The breeze coming in from the open doors didn't cool off the heat singeing Kenzie's cheeks.

"If I didn't want to avoid making my date think I was a crazy lady, I would have whistled at the two of you."

Glad to see her aunt was returning to a normal, sober state, Kenzie sat back in her seat. "Maybe you're the one who needs to start talking. Who is the man I saw you churning ice cream with at The Scoop?"

Aunt Jody waved her hand and shook her head. "I see the way you're trying to change the subject. Let's just call it even. I won't ask you anything, and you don't ask me."

"Sounds like a deal to me."

The cryptic conversation stayed with Kenzie as she walked around the ballroom looking for Ramon. Something Auntie Bren had said stuck with her, too. A month ago she'd made plans with Rafael to attend the gala. She chose Rafael because he was safe. She didn't want anything other than to have someone to attend important functions with. Like Ramon reminded her the other night, although she never agreed to his proposal, he still came through for her.

Kenzie spotted Ramon by the bar talking to the mayor and Alexander, along with what could only be Ramon's brother. Judging from the wrinkles in Ramon's forehead and the scowl across his face, he was not pleased. She wouldn't be, either, if she had to talk to those two. He needed rescuing. She gathered her heavy skirts in her hands and set off.

"Kenzie, dear?"

The accented voice belonged to Ana Torres. When Kenzie looked in the direction of where her name was called, she saw Mrs. Torres, who wore a shimmering floor-length silver gown. Her dark hair was pulled up in a fancy bun with baby's breath sprinkled throughout her locks. Like Ramon and everyone in his family she was tall and lean in stature. When they'd talked in the bookstore Kenzie had figured who she was but didn't want to let on. Now, since Ramon had given her a giant kiss in front of everyone, she feared his mother might have some words for her. Would she approve?

"Mrs. Torres." Kenzie gulped, her eyes averted toward Ramon. The bewildered smile on his face made her smile.

"Ana, please," Ramon's mother corrected. "I was just going over there to bring the boys back to the table when I saw you over here. Julio is the mayor back home and he can talk shop all night long to people."

"I can imagine," Kenzie said with a nod. Though they'd both been heading in the same direction the two ladies stood there for a moment. "Are you enjoying Southwood?"

"I am." Ana beamed. "I plan on going back to the bookstore to get some more of that lovely tea we had today."

Kenzie patted Ana's arm. "I already arranged a box to be sent to your room."

"So sweet!" Ana leaned over and hugged Kenzie. "No wonder my son is in love with you."

The word *love* weakened Kenzie's knees.

Ana tugged her silver shawl around her arms. "Don't look so surprised."

"Ramon and I are just figuring things out," Kenzie responded nervously.

"I don't think Ramon needs any figuring," said Ana, "or he wouldn't have kissed you like that in front of his whole family."

Of course she'd seen it. Who hadn't? Kenzie searched for the words to say. Luckily a set of arms wrapped around her waist. Ramon pressed his lips against Kenzie's neck. "Sorry to interrupt, Ma, but I need to steal my lady for a moment."

"Of course," said Ana. "But Kenzie, you have to promise to come over to the hotel tomorrow for brunch. My daughter-in-law, Grace, is going to teach Ramon's chef how to cook."

"Jessilyn is a fine chef," said Ramon, squeezing Kenzie's body against his.

"You're thin," Ana countered and turned to Kenzie. "He must have lost at least twenty pounds since you brought Philly home. Kenzie, will you come tomorrow?"

"I would be honored, Ana."

"And please bring your family, too. Oh look." She sighed. "Julio will talk that poor mayor's ear off. Let me go get him."

Finally alone together, at least as much as two people could be at a gala event, Kenzie turned in Ramon's arms. First and foremost he kissed her lips, giving a little suck to her bottom lip where she'd placed her lipstick a few moments ago.

"How long before we can leave?" Ramon asked.

"We," Kenzie said, wagging her finger between his chest and her breast, "can't leave together. Not tonight."

"What? Why?"

"Because your folks are in town and you need to spend time with them, and I think my aunt Jody might stay at my place this evening."

Ramon bent down and pressed his forehead against hers. "This isn't how I envisioned the evening going for us."

"Let me guess, it had something to do with stripping out of our clothes?" Kenzie asked. They swayed to the melody played by the DJ.

"Lady, with that dress you have on, nothing needs to come off." He jokingly pushed his hips forward. "Since we can't spend the night with each other, how about we go find ourselves an elevator?"

Confused, Kenzie narrowed her eyes. "But every time we get on one…" When she glanced up he wiggled his brows. What a shame they were on the ground floor. "You're crazy, you know that? No wonder I am falling in love with you." The words just fell out. Kenzie held her breath, shocked.

"That's definitely going to get me through the night." Ramon kissed her, deeply. "I love you too, Kenzie."

"Ramon," Ana cooed the following morning. "I am in love with Kenzie Swayne."

You and me both, Ramon thought to himself. He offered a simple smile to his mother and a gentle squeeze of her hand.

They stood on one side of the brunch table as Kenzie and her family came down the walkway of Magnolia Palace. Silver cloches covered the dishes but not the delicious rich and sweet smells. Ramon's stomach ached for food while his heart ached for Kenzie. Two whole nights without her were too many.

"You aren't the slightest bit uncomfortable with the Swaynes coming over here for breakfast?" His brother Julio asked, watching the family come closer. "Wasn't this their family home? And now you're bringing them here because you're sleeping with their daughter?"

"Awkward." Raul laughed under his breath but loud enough for the family to hear.

"Both of you, shut up," ordered their father.

Ramon gave a silent thanks for one of the few times his father stood up for him. It never occurred to Ramon this morning might be awkward for Kenzie's whole family until Julio had opened his mouth.

If the Swaynes were upset, they didn't show it. Maggie held her phone out, recording herself and occasionally spinning around in panoramic fashion. Everyone wore something in the white or beige family. The men wore light-colored beachcomber linen pants and button-down linen shirts. The ladies all wore one form of sundress or another. Kenzie covered the top of her head with a wide-brimmed hat. He would kill to hide behind the hat and kiss her right now.

Ramon had met Kenzie's niece, Bailey, earlier this week. Bailey's father looked very much like Kenzie's dad. The apple didn't fall far from the tree. The main difference between father and son was that in the summer light, Richard's hair had a red tint. Another woman, not Kenzie's mother, linked her arm with Kenzie's. Ramon wondered if Paula Hairston-Swayne had decided to skip brunch. Was it because she thought Kenzie had sided with him instead of Erin on the building? Surely not.

"Mr. Swayne." Ramon came around his side of the table with his hand stretched out for a shake.

"Ramon, we discussed this—call me Mitch."

Ramon cast a glance over his shoulder at his parents. "I needed them to know that it was okay with you."

"Though his hair may look it, he wasn't raised in a barn," said Ramon's father.

Mitch chuckled and shook hands with everyone from the Torres and Reyes families. "Mitch Swayne," he said to Julio Senior.

"Julio Senior, and this is my wife, Ana. It is a pleasure to meet you."

"Thanks. Thanks for having us today, Ramon."

The dark-haired woman beside Mitch cleared her throat. "Oh, where are my manners? These are my daughters. Kenzie, you all know, and my oldest daughter, Magnolia. We call her Maggie."

Maggie paused to stop live-streaming herself. "Really, Dad? That's how you want to introduce me?"

"I could introduce you as my narcissistic daughter?" Mitch suggested.

"Uh, I am working." Maggie rolled her eyes and went back to her camera.

Mitch shook his head and continued his introductions *Family Feud* style. "My daughter considers being popular a job. But anyway, this is my lovely granddaughter Bailey and her father, my son, Richard."

Richard shook hands with everyone.

"And beside me is my sister, Jody Lynn."

"Jody's just fine," Jody said, stepping forward.

Ramon always thought Kenzie favored her mother but even with the dark hair on Jody, Ramon saw the family resemblance through and through with the heart-shaped face and high cheekbones.

"I love what you've done with the place." Jody gaped.

"Thank you," said Ramon. Kenzie came and stood by his side. He straightened to his full height with pride. "I'll have to give you the tour."

"Don't you think they already know what the place looks like?" Julio asked with a scowl.

"We never lived here," said Richard, putting everyone at ease. "This place once belonged to a distant relative."

"This sounds fascinating," Ana said, waving her hands over the magnolia table-scape. "Please sit. We have a variety of things, some fresh baked Mallorca bread, *pastelón*, and of course grits and eggs. We'll eat while you tell us more about your Magnolia Palace."

Ramon and Kenzie sat together. As Richard told the story of Magnolia Palace, Kenzie held Ramon's hand under the table. The simple touch of her thumb sliding over the top of his hand was such a turn-on. He was pretty sure no one would appreciate it if he pushed everything off the table and made love to her until the sun set.

"The house was really just a frame when it was constructed. My sister loves to paint Southwood as some Norman Rockwell city but even after the Civil War, most Black people lived in the city limits. There were still former Confederates who terrorized the town. To live outside the city limits was rare. Many homes were set on fire, including this one. Each time, the frame stood." Richard went on. "Ramon's done a fantastic job remodeling."

"Speaking of remodeling," his brother Julio said, "congratulations on your new spot downtown. Are you going to turn that into a bed-and-breakfast?"

"Not now, Julio," Jose said over his mimosa. His wife, Grace, pulled his hand under the table.

Julio looked between his brothers. "What? I can't ask my little brother a question?"

"If he wanted to talk about it," said Jose, "he would have brought it up to you. There was a reason that mayor's assistant came to you to tell you about the place."

As a US Marshal, Jose was suspicious of everyone. Usually he wasn't wrong and considering Ramon figured the mayor's assistant in question was probably Alexander, Jose was certainly right about this.

"I haven't decided," Ramon answered honestly.

"We were talking about making it a tutoring place or hangout for kids." Kenzie looked over at him with adoration. Ramon winced, recalling the ideas Anson breezed by him last night.

"Yeah, instead of having them trespassing on the property for thrills." Ramon chuckled nervously.

"That sounds like a great idea." Jody beamed.

"It sounds like you won't be making a profit," Julio sneered. A bang from under the table shook the pitchers of tea and magnolia vases. "Ouch."

"Sorry," Lexi said, sitting back from her seat and rubbing her protruding belly. "I never know when this one is going to up and decide to kick me."

"Well, maybe it's a sign we put an end to the subject of Ramon's potential business," said Raul. "Because I am going to work on him for a nightclub."

"Fat chance," Julio said, then scooted out of the way before Lexi had a chance to kick him again. "All right, I'm dropping the subject."

"Bailey, thank you so much for being able to make it to brunch with us." Ana leaned over. "I understand you'll be sequestered at Brutti Hotel for the week because of a beauty pageant thing?"

"Yes, ma'am," Bailey answered shyly. "I check in this afternoon."

Kimber started to speak at the same time as Lexi. Lexi nodded for Kimber to explain. "They do that so the girls can work on a group dance and practice walking on the stage. Tía Amelia." She paused for approval from the family. Once everyone nodded and smiled, she continued. "She has contacts from her old job at MET who are going to get some footage."

Multi-Ethnic Television was a staple channel in every household, especially in Villa San Juan. Ramon and his family religiously watched *Azúcar*, a popular reality show featuring the Ruiz family from Puerto Rico. The Torres-Reyes family had a former producer in their family now. Seated by her husband, Amelia nodded to confirm. "That's right. The world loves beauty pageants. Are you nervous, Bailey?"

"Oh yes, ma'am," Bailey answered with a soft giggle as she tucked her light red hair behind her ear.

The teenager reminded Ramon of Kenzie. He wondered— if they had a child, would she look like Bailcy or at least have the Hairston red hair? Ramon glanced over at Kenzie and smiled.

"Cool," said Kimber. "I would love to come hang out

with you backstage. I know it can become crazy over there. It's nice having a friendly face with you, and since we're practically family... Ouch."

"Sorry," Lexi blurted out. She flipped her blond ponytail over her shoulder. "The baby just keeps kicking me today."

Judging from the red blush on Kenzie's face, she got the gist of the reason for Lexi's outburst. Marriage. Kenzie had made it perfectly clear she wasn't interested in that. She also said she didn't want him to escort her to any events, yet they were together all the time. Being with Kenzie felt natural. The problems from last year were gone. He always looked forward to seeing her and couldn't wait to be with her, even if they were apart for an hour. Damn, was he really ready for this step? Hell yes. Was she? Ramon wondered if a true proposal would get her to say yes.

The conversation switched to beauty pageants. Ramon squeezed Kenzie's hand. Alexander's discovery haunted him. Jody had bragged about Kenzie's win, and how the family tradition would be carried on in the beauty queen world. If it ever got out Kenzie wasn't the true queen, he didn't know what she'd do. The pride in her eyes killed him. The last thing he wanted to do was take this away from her.

Chapter 11

"Ladies and gentlemen." Kenzie tapped her silver sparkled nails against the microphone. The color, Winning by Ravens Cosmetics, was a special edition polish in honor of the Miss Southwood Beauty Pageant. Tradition brought an employee of the cosmetics company to Southwood to sit on the panel as a judge for this year's bunch of contestants. Last year they sent CEO Will Ravens, who at the time had been a newcomer to the cosmetics world. Kenzie was honored to witness the budding relationship between Will and beauty aficionado Zoe Baldwin, now Zoe Ravens. This year they sent Will's brother, Donovan Ravens, the CFO. Like Will, Donovan looked just as uncomfortable sitting on the designated judges' area as the ladies seated next to him. Donovan scowled, looking like a grumpy bear with his arms folded across his chest, clearly not in the mood for the festivities. Kenzie worried that his awkwardness was already rubbing off on the judges, and it might reflect in their scoring.

Kenzie smiled and waved at the crowd in the theater in downtown Southwood. She stood on the same stage where she'd won years ago. "Are we having a great time tonight?"

The crowd responded with a cheer.

"Well, I don't want to keep everyone here longer than need be because we have one killer party tonight, don't we?"

Another roar came from the audience.

"All right, without further ado, let's bring on this year's ladies and they'll all tell you who's sponsoring them."

Each year local businesses sponsored a contestant. Everyone wore a sash promoting their respective business. Waverly insisted Bailey wear last year's sash, sponsored by Crowne Restorations.

Kenzie stood off to the side of the stage just behind the curtains. Aunt Jody wrapped her arms around her shoulders.

"Can I tell you how proud I am of you?"

"Thanks, Aunt Jody," Kenzie said, beaming. "I wouldn't be here without your support."

"Yes, I know."

There was something strange about the way Aunt Jody answered. Kenzie inhaled just to make sure she didn't smell alcohol on her aunt's breath. Last week during brunch, Aunt Jody really put back the mimosas. Granted, they were delicious with the twist of mango juice from Ana's mango tree back home.

"I can't thank you enough for being here for Bailey," said Kenzie, patting Aunt Jody's arm.

"I was here for yours."

The confession caught Kenzie off guard. "What?"

Aunt Jody let Kenzie go and stepped backward. She wore a black knee-length gown and a magnolia tucked behind her ear. "I was. I just didn't want your stank mother to see me."

Kenzie rolled her eyes. "It was bad enough she didn't come to the brunch because you were coming."

"It was a family brunch," Aunt Jody said in a clipped tone. "A Swayne brunch. She's not a Swayne."

"Aunt Jody," Kenzie huffed. "This feud is going on long enough. Mom is right over there," she said, pointing to the front row, where her mother sat with her eyes glued to Bailey at the microphone.

"I wonder if I can throw something at her."

"Even if you could, I wouldn't let you. She's still my mom."

Aunt Jody patted Kenzie on the shoulder. "And I'm sorry for that, dear. Oh look, here comes Bailey now."

It wasn't difficult to quickly plaster on a smile. Bailey made Kenzie smile with pride. Her hair was teased high and combed back like a traditional beauty queen's. "You were so great out there."

Tears welled in Bailey's eyes. "Are you sure? I feel so silly like this."

"If you didn't feel silly, you wouldn't be doing it right, sweetie," Aunt Jody offered.

"Ignore her, okay?"

Other girls exited the stage. Kenzie tried not to show too much favoritism. Being an aunt of one of the contestants prohibited Kenzie from being an emcee but she was given a few responsibilities at the beginning, middle and end. The end was where she fully expected to pass the torch. Kenzie even brought the crown she'd worn ten years ago to place on top of Bailey's head.

"Do I really have to do 'Singing in the Rain'?" Bailey asked.

"What other number do you know?" Kenzie asked her. "We've only been practicing for weeks now."

"I know, but still." Bailey chewed on her bottom lip.

"It's just nerves," Aunt Jody offered, placing her hands on Bailey's shoulder as a coach would for a nervous player.

Suddenly Kenzie felt guilty. She thought about what Erin had said to her, about how beauty pageants were her whole. Was Erin right?

"Probably," Bailey mumbled.

"Bailey," Kenzie said. The emcee announced the bathing suit portion. Some of the other girls who had walked off stage before Bailey were now lining up behind the curtain. Kenzie remembered the excitement. She lived for it. What did Erin know? "Bailey, if you're unsure, you don't have to do this."

"What?" Aunt Jody gasped. "Of course she does."

"No, she doesn't, Aunt Jody," Kenzie said, stepping in front of her aunt so Bailey could only focus on her. "If you want to walk away right now, there's nothing wrong with it. I'll go get the car."

"No," said Bailey, shaking her head. "I want to do it."

"See?" Aunt Jody said smugly. "Let her go change."

"I'll walk with you," Kenzie said, linking her arm in the crook of Bailey's elbow. Aunt Jody hip checked Kenzie and took her place beside Bailey. "Aunt Jody!"

"Sorry, dear," said Aunt Jody over her shoulder as they walked away, "I don't trust you to keep her mind on the tiara."

"Crazy lady." Kenzie laughed to herself and shook her head. Turning back to the swimsuit portion of the event, she folded her arms across her chest and sighed in relief, still glad Bailey decided to stay in the competition.

A set of brown hands wrapped around her arms. "Reminds you of some old times, doesn't it?"

Kenzie jerked forward, hitting the curtains. "What is wrong with you, Alexander?" Immediately she wiped the spot of her skin he'd touched.

"What?" Alexander had the nerve to blink innocently.

"You can't tell me all this doesn't bring up memories of when we were together."

"Yes, I exactly can," Kenzie snapped.

"Remember how we stood backstage waiting to do your number?"

"You mean how you flaked on me and Hank had to step in and help me?" Kenzie countered.

Alexander at least had the decency to look ashamed. "Sorry. I was trying to bring up the good times in our past."

"That's exactly what they are, Alexander. The past."

Alexander tugged at the knot of his green paisley tie. "Is this because of the long-haired freak you've been seeing?"

"Ramon?"

"Don't say his name like you don't know who I'm talking about, Kenzie."

Kenzie shook her head from side to side. "I don't know where this strange nostalgia and this burst of inappropriate jealousy are coming from but they stop now. You had your chance ten years ago, and you had the last six months to approach me correctly, but you weren't man enough then. Don't start now."

"You think your new man is so perfect?"

Hands down, Kenzie thought, Ramon was the best thing in her life. She'd realized this week how she'd kept her heart guarded ever since her breakup with Alexander. Kenzie didn't plan on wallowing in her what-ifs with other men she dated in the past. She focused on the exhilarating feeling she experienced every time she and Ramon were together. "He's better than you."

Kenzie cast a glance from behind the curtain at where Ramon sat between Maggie and Richard. Her heart swelled with pride. Their families blended beautifully together.

The contestants entered and exited the stage in a crisscross fashion. The girls under eighteen wore peach-colored, one-piece bathing suits and flip-flops. The older ladies wore whatever, bikinis, tankinis or one-pieces, with or without heels.

As the girls stepped off stage, Kenzie moved closer to the curtains to keep from being trampled. The next event was the talent portion and Kenzie had the honor of introducing this part.

"He's no better than me," Alexander sneered.

"He is."

"Cute. Well, just hang tight." Alexander grabbed Kenzie by the wrist and tugged her on the stage. The audience, unaware of the tension, clapped as expected. Kenzie focused on the red light of the camera from the television studio. When she'd competed a decade ago, no one had filmed it.

"Ladies and gentlemen," Alexander said into the microphone, "it's a pleasure being here tonight. I don't know about you but I'm enjoying myself. How about you?" Alexander took the microphone off the stand and faced Kenzie, giving her such a smug smile she felt nauseous.

"I know we're doing things different this year, inviting everyone from all four points to enter, but how many of you were here ten years ago when my beautiful companion standing here with me won her crown?"

The crowd answered with applause. Kenzie glanced around, not sure where Alexander was going with this.

"Well, who can believe this beautiful beauty queen grew up to become Dr. Mackenzie Swayne? She's our town historian and she's helping Southwood stay honest to its true form. Why, in fact, she recently spoke to our economics committee about restoring some of our buildings, keeping their integrity and all that smart stuff." Alexander pressed his hand to his chest. "I'm not as bright as Dr. Swayne, but I get her part about keeping up the integrity. So can you imagine my surprise when her current boyfriend, Ramon Torres, the same man who went behind her family's back and bought their historic home, made an offer to the committee we couldn't pass up?"

The crowd hesitated in their applause, also unsure of where Alexander was going with this rant. Kenzie glanced out into the crowd to find Ramon. His seat between her siblings was now empty. "Well, I'm glad to make this announcement with the residents of Black Wolf Creek, Peachville and Samaritan here in the same audience. After meeting with Ramon's people and some of the builders I've used in the past, Ramon's new venture, a sports bar and club, will open downtown next month, and I guarantee all of you are invited to the grand opening."

Kenzie cocked her head to the side, sure she was not hearing correctly.

Proud of himself, Alexander winked. "How's that for integrity?" he asked her with a devious chuckle and glare, but spoke into the microphone. A scuffle sounded off behind her. The curtains shifted and when they steadied, Anson and a few men in blue jackets with the word Security written in yellow, stood in front of Ramon, blocking him from coming onto the stage.

"Oh, and speaking of integrity," Alexander went on, "Ramon and I discovered a box of ballots from ten years ago from this very competition. It seems someone threw out a ridiculous amount of votes, votes that would have assured my sister, Felicia Ward—" he chuckled and shook his head "—Felicia Crawford, received the winning crown."

Over her internal screams, the crowd gasped. Everyone stared at Kenzie. Vertigo set in. Her body swayed. She blinked in disbelief as the news began to sink in. Her legs moved on autopilot, turning in Ramon's direction. Anson released him and he ran toward her.

"Kenzie."

"You knew the ballots were from my pageant?" Her voice choked out in a hoarse whisper. "How long have you known?"

"Kenzie, let's go…"

"How long?" Kenzie screamed. The theater was as quiet as a church mouse.

Ramon scratched the back of his head. "Since the gala."

"The gala was a week ago." Hot tears threatened her eyes. "You could have said something."

"I—"

She pushed his chest. "No, you don't get to say anything now. You knew and you could have said something. Instead you allowed Alexander—" She hiccupped a sob. "You let Alexander of all people be the one to let me know." She felt like such a fool. Her biggest claim to Southwood fame was winning her pageant and now it was lost. Humiliation didn't begin to describe her feelings. She had failed her family and their legacy.

Aunt Jody came out of nowhere, wrapping her arm around Kenzie and guiding her off the stage. For the first time in her life, Kenzie held her head low and slunk away. Once she reached the curtains, Richard stood there waiting for her. Then she fainted.

"Ramon, dear."

Ramon glanced up from his third chocolate cupcake to the hand on his fitted white shirt. He wiped his hands on the back of his jeans and stood up to greet Auntie Bren. The sight of the red hair on the matriarch's head caused Ramon's heart to pulse. Two days had passed since he'd been double-crossed by Alexander Ward. He put a lot of blame on Julio as well for indulging Alexander's ideas of what kind of business to put in the old building. Julio gave the misguided impression to Alexander that he could talk him into anything. Ramon never agreed to anything and now he spent his time turning down venders Julio sent over. Right now Ramon didn't want to have anything to do with the building, not if it was going to cost him Kenzie.

Since the shop had opened, he'd been sitting in The Cupcakery, hoping to get a glance of Kenzie leaving her apartment or walking through downtown Southwood. It was Tuesday, dreaded Tuesday, and Kenzie still hadn't returned his calls. He hadn't heard from her nor seen her in forty-eight hours.

A billow of steam from his fifth coffee floated up and met a disapproving gaze.

"Auntie Bren." Ramon tried to say her name with a smile. It didn't feel right.

"What are you doing sitting here all by yourself?"

Ramon lifted a brow. Had she been under a rock for the last few days? "Just enjoying a cupcake."

"What do you have?" Auntie Bren peered over Ramon's table. "Mmm, Devastating Decadent Chocolate? And three wrappers?"

Guiltily, Ramon nodded his head. "Yep." He owned it. Who said only women drowned themselves in food? Men did, too. And Ramon was miserable.

"May I?" Auntie Bren motioned toward the empty seat in front of the stack of paperwork he'd been signing all morning long for the renovations of the post office.

Ramon expected Auntie Bren to ask about the building. People stopped Ramon in the streets to ask about his plans. Just this morning someone had offered to share his winnings from the bet going on from the local bowling team. Ramon had plans, all right—ones that were going to blow Kenzie away and prove to her he'd been listening. Right now the front of the building remained covered by plywood. Construction went around the clock. Keeping the structure of the building intact was going to cost Ramon a fortune. When Ramon delivered his check to the bank he learned the main reason the council had backed him was because Erin Hairston would have had to build an outside ramp to accommodate her patients and that would have changed the exterior structure. Ramon had a side entrance he could make wheelchair accessible that Erin wouldn't have been able to.

Auntie Bren raised a manicured finger at the counter. Ramon turned to see who her dining partner was and caught a glimpse of the man from the Ward wedding, Oscar something.

"I have you to thank for my temporary boyfriend."

Great, he thought. At least someone got a relationship out of this month. "Congratulations," Ramon said.

"Well, he isn't really *new*," Auntie Bren went on to say. "Nor is he really a boyfriend. I just like saying the word. I'm breaking things off when I leave for Miami next week."

"You two look so happy together." Prior to Auntie Bren coming over to visit him, he'd seen the two walking down the street, heading toward The Cupcakery. Ramon had observed the chivalrous way Oscar caught a kid whizzing by on a bicycle with his cane after the boy cut between them as they held hands. Ramon could only assume Oscar had made the boy apologize because the kid had gotten off his bike and held out his hand for Auntie Bren to shake. Ramon had kept his head low when he realized they were heading into the cupcake shop. It was bad enough he'd run into what had to have been every other Swayne and Hairston family member in town, who had all felt the need to tell him off.

Snickering, Auntie Bren shook her head. "Oscar and I

are familiar with each other. We were sweethearts before he went off to the war."

Which one? he thought.

"When he left, I walked down to the old post office every day and mailed him a letter. I handed them to my best gal pal, Priscilla." Auntie Bren cut her eyes over at the counter and half smiled at Oscar. "He claimed he wrote me one as well, but I never received it."

"I'm sorry to hear that. I assume because you never heard from each other, you fell apart and never saw each other again."

"No, not exactly. I went to visit my family up north in Chicago when he returned from the Korean War—yes, baby, he was a career military man. I came back and I saw him. Saw him with my best gal pal."

The math caught up with Ramon. He pressed his lips together when he realized Oscar's dirty deed. There was no ghost in the old post office. Oscar did exactly what Ramon had tried to tell Kenzie. He was a player.

"I couldn't stand seeing him with someone else, especially when I thought he and I had been so in love, so I moved away. I rarely ever come back to Southwood because I don't want to run into him."

The story sounded vaguely familiar. Kenzie was avoiding him. Unlike Oscar, Ramon had an excuse. Alexander was a liar. A liar with a broken nose now, but still a liar. Ramon clenched his fist. Ramon didn't want another day to go by without talking to Kenzie, let alone a half a century. Right now she refused to see him.

"And here you are with him."

"Sure, for now." Auntie Bren shrugged her shoulders. The knot of her purple sweater shifted and she tugged it back down toward the center of her purple-and-white plaid shirt.

"Auntie Bren, we've known each other for a while," he began with a teasing smile, "so I am sure you're here to give me comforting words of support."

"No, dear, if I wanted to do that, I'd tell you to get off your ass and go make things right with my niece." She reached out and smacked Ramon on the back of his head. "She snuck out of her apartment this morning and is at her office. But you better do something grand to win her back."

"Yes, ma'am."

"These came for you."

Kenzie looked up from her office to find another dozen roses in a glass vase so big they covered Margaret's face from her view. Without looking at the card, Kenzie shook her head.

"No thank you."

"Kenzie," Margaret began, holding the crystal vase at her hip, "you've only been in the office for two hours and already this is the second dozen he's sent today, and while I'm no mathematician, I can only guess there will be six dozen more to come if you stay the rest of the day."

"Then it's a good thing I am working a half day today."

Roses had been delivered every hour on the hour to her apartment. Everyone in her complex received a batch. Did Ramon think flowers were going to smooth things over? He lied to her, not so much about the business but knowing about the missing votes. Losing the Miss Southwood title like that, in such an embarrassing way, devastated her. Sure, her world had not ended and her friends were supportive but the idea still hurt her. And Ramon knew. Anger bubbled inside of her for thinking about it. She stared at Margaret, who waited for an answer. Kenzie guessed today's batches could be split and sent over to the two senior centers.

The only reason Kenzie came into the office today was to collect the box she'd left there. Waverly's surprise wedding was later on today and after that Kenzie planned on going to the family cabin in Black Wolf Creek. Kenzie had informed Dario and Darren Crowne that she had no plans to attend the wedding but she would stop by at the reception to show her face.

After Kenzie gave the instructions for the roses, Margaret shook her head and mumbled something under her breath about appreciating gifts. Clearly Margaret hadn't been at the Miss Southwood Beauty Pageant two days ago. *So what?* Kenzie thought to herself. Eventually the whole town would know.

The tiny office smelled like fresh flowers. How did he even know she'd come into work today? Kenzie hadn't bothered mentioning it to anyone she'd be coming in, except for Alexander's secretary.

Left alone with her thoughts, Kenzie almost wished she hadn't come in at all. The elevator ride up to her office involved a lot of pats on her back and words of encouragement such as *tough break*, *hang in there* and *God always has a reason why*.

And even with those well-wishers, Kenzie still faced the scrutiny of those who thought she personally cheated or at least conspired to cheat. Felicia called from her honeymoon in Barbados to say no hard feelings and it meant nothing to her now. But it meant everything to Kenzie. She wasn't a cheater. And then there was her family. Everyone wanted to know who rigged the vote. Kenzie didn't know if that mattered now.

Aunt Jody showed her true devotion to the bottle. She didn't even bother mixing her vodka with orange juice or tomato juice, or even a glass. From the time Kenzie received the news she was no longer a winner, Aunt Jody stayed by Kenzie's side, even when her mother, Paula, came over.

The two ladies put their differences aside to take care of Kenzie. Not that she wanted help. Her father, Mitch, tried to reassure her that no matter what, she would always be his princess. As much as it killed her to stay away, Kenzie didn't want Bailey to see her like this. And no one wanted to talk about Sunday's results. Kenzie preferred to be left alone and no one seemed to take the hint, not even Maggie.

"There you are!"

Kenzie blinked to get her eyes to focus and found her sister standing in the doorway, hair piled on top of her head like a mop with a gardenia tucked behind her ear. She wore a peach-colored dress. Meanwhile, Kenzie, dressed in the same pair of sweats since Sunday night, stepped forward.

"Why are you here?" Kenzie snapped.

"Why are *you* here?" Maggie clapped back. "You're off work this month. Or did you forget? You took this month off for all the weddings and events."

Kenzie shuffled some paperwork around to seem busy. "Yeah, well, everything is over with, so I might as well get to it."

Maggie waltzed farther into the office and perched herself on the edge of Kenzie's desk. "You have one more wedding to attend."

"Since it is a *surprise* wedding for Waverly, she won't even know I was supposed to be in it. Besides, of all people, Waverly will understand," said Kenzie. Waverly had suffered from internet bullying and was publicly mocked when she lost one beauty queen title before becoming Miss Southwood. Kenzie didn't bother checking social media. She woke up every night in sweats remembering the red light on the *live* camera from Multi-Ethnic Television. "Dominic said it wasn't formal."

Maggie rolled her eyes. "I've met her mother. It's going to be formal."

"Jillian Leverve just wants to see her daughter married before the baby is born," Kenzie explained and went back to shuffling her papers. "They don't need me there for that."

One minute Kenzie was tapping the papers in her hands to a beat and the next her hands were empty. Maggie snatched the documents and held the work over the edge of the desk and sprinkled the papers into the wastebasket.

"Go away, Maggie."

"Not without you."

"I don't want to be around people."

Maggie sighed. "I noticed your luggage is missing from your closet."

Kenzie let asking her sister why she was in her closet slide. "I'm going to the cabin."

"Smart. I'll be there."

"I don't need company," Kenzie said.

"I'm not just company." Maggie pouted. "I'm your sister. How long do you want to stay?"

Snarling, Kenzie shrugged. Did she stay for as long as it took Ramon to build his sports bar? She didn't want to pass by the building every day and see it being ruined, littered with sports paraphernalia, loud games and drunk fans? How had she ever thought Ramon matured? He'd looked her in the eyes and lied. Red-hot anger boiled in her veins. She wasn't sure she'd ever want to see him again. But forever wasn't an option. "A while."

"Long enough to wait out the sports bar?"

If she said she didn't care, Kenzie knew her sister would know she was lying. Instead she answered, "We'll see."

"Well, have you read any of the cards Ramon sent?"

Heart aching, Kenzie wondered if it was time to ban

his name from being said. "I don't want to have anything to do with him."

"A week ago you were in love with him," Maggie reminded Kenzie. "Don't be like Auntie Bren. I took the liberty of reading his cards."

Of course you did. Kenzie stewed.

"He never agreed to build a sports bar. That was Anson and Ramon's brother Julio, who were talking mayor talk. They came up with the idea. You know all it takes is a little inkling for Alexander to find out something bothers you and then he runs with it."

"I don't care about the building," Kenzie interrupted her sister. The words choked her. Ramon had failed her. Again. Now, instead of being humiliated in front of a small group of people, the whole world got to see the moment she was proclaimed a fraudulent beauty queen. He'd promised never to humiliate her and had failed. Again.

"It looks like a florist exploded in here, too," said Maggie, changing the subject.

Kenzie half smiled. "At least the flowers will brighten up the senior centers."

"Aw, there's my baby sis," Maggie cooed. "Do you want to go visit there? That always makes you happy, talking to the lifelong residents of Southwood."

"No," Kenzie said, shaking her head. "I just wanted to grab a few things before going to the cabin. I can't take being at my apartment with Aunt Jody there. And Mom."

"Yeah, they're killing me with kindness toward each other. This morning I saw each of them insisting on the other taking the last lemon cupcake."

"Sir." Margaret's voice carried into Kenzie's office. "Sir!"

The only thing Kenzie could do was stand up. Her chair hit the back of her wall and jutted forward, hitting her behind the knees. She fell back into her seat when Ramon appeared in her doorway. His hair hung loose and surrounded his face and fell down the front of his white shirt. Kenzie hated herself for her body's reaction to the sight of him in his form-fitting jeans. Hopefully, the way she sighed covered her desire. Maggie slid off Kenzie's desk in an attempt to put herself between Ramon and her sister.

"Maggie, I've come to adore you like a sister but right now you need to move."

"No," said Maggie, folding her arms across the peach bodice of her dress. "I'm not going to let you hurt her."

Ramon tossed Kenzie a look. Her heart seized in her chest. "Kenzie, seriously?"

Kenzie lifted her chin. Margaret stood behind him, talking to someone on the other end of her cell phone, giving them the full description of what the "intruder," as she put it, wore.

"Kenzie, you know I'd never knowingly hurt you."

She hated the way his voice pleaded as if he were in pain. Well, she was in pain, too. "Just leave me alone, Ramon." Kenzie turned around in her chair, scraping her knees against the wall.

A static noise from the radio of an approaching security officer sliced through the tension of the room. "Kenzie," Ramon said. "At least look at me."

For some reason she obeyed, spinning back around. Three security officers tried to grab his arms. Ramon pulled away. "I meant it when I said I'd never do anything to jeopardize us."

"I recall you saying you weren't going to hurt me," Kenzie replied coolly. She smoothed her hands against the top of her desk. Her bare fingertips brushed against the leftover box from the basement of the post office. "You knew about the votes."

"Yes, I knew," said Ramon. He pulled away from the security guards and advanced closer. Kenzie pressed her back into her seat. "I made the choice not to say anything to you. I thought Alexander wanted to keep it quiet, as well."

"You thought?" Kenzie squinted her eyes. "By going along with whatever Alexander came up with, you humiliated me. Was it for the seat at the big kids' table? You wanted to be on the local committees so bad you were willing to compromise me?"

"It's not like you think."

"What I think is you knew how he humiliated me before."

"It was the lesser of two evils, Kenzie." Ramon exhaled.

"Well, you chose poorly." Kenzie sniffled. She'd thought she was done crying. "You promised me. You promised you would never humiliate me."

"I didn't."

"You did," she said with a simple smile. "Again."

"Kenzie, if you're not going to talk to me…" he said, coming closer.

"Sir," a security guard said.

Ignoring them, Ramon clamped his hands down on the arms of her chair. He leaned his head close; his sweet breath smelled like chocolate cupcakes. His dark eyes were black, scary black, as they searched her face. Kenzie shut her eyes but he jerked her chair to get her attention.

"I knew you were going to hurt me," Kenzie clipped.

Ramon bowed his head for a moment then looked back at her. The whites of his eyes turned red. "Then you came into this relationship with the cards already stacked against me."

"I want him out of here!" someone screamed.

"What the hell happened to you?" Kenzie heard Maggie question someone outside the door. She and Ramon locked eyes, neither of them blinking. Finally he nodded and stood up, grabbing the box from the post office off her desk. "I'm out of here. I just came to get what's mine."

Once the doors to the stairwell stopped rattling after Ramon stormed out the side exit, Kenzie breathed. She blinked to get her eyes to focus and her brows drew together. Alexander was just outside her door, dressed for work in a suit, but also with one of those nose guards basketball players wear. That, however, hadn't protected him from a flying ball or elbow. It had been too late for that. Deep puffy purple circles were under his eyes.

"Don't worry, he won't be bothering you anymore," Alexander said nasally. "I'm in the process of filing a restraining order against him after he punched me at the pageant."

Finally able to push away from her desk, Kenzie stood up. "I quit."

Chapter 12

Even though Kenzie had quit a month ago, her connections to Southwood High School kept her in good standing to serve on the Christmas Advisory Council. She thought staying in Black Wolf Creek, hiding out, would heal her wounds. But now that she found herself standing outside of the old post office, doubts washed over her. Kenzie bit her bottom lip and glanced up at the building. Whatever name Ramon planned to give the sports bar was covered with a thick white sheet. His clout or whatever he'd bartered got the first meeting for the Christmas Advisory Council held on the same day as his soft opening; the meetings were traditionally held in City Hall, and had been for decades, since Southwood had decided to welcome out-of-towners to experience the holidays in a small town. Shops donated money and items to help make each year grander than the one before.

"You okay?"

Beside her, Maggie linked her arm through Kenzie's and forced a smile onto her face instead of lying. Her heart raced. Her legs shook in her three-inch sandals. Thank God the bright yellow scoop-necked dress she wore covered her legs. Kenzie linked her sister's arm with her own and looked both ways. "Is that our parents' car?"

Maggie followed Kenzie's glance. "I think so. Mama said something to me in a text about coming to more meetings."

"You don't have to be here to babysit me, you know."

"I know, but Southwood is my home."

Kenzie raised a brow at her sister. "You may have been with me for the last month but I know you're ready to be with your followers."

"Does this mean I don't have to wait on you hand and foot?"

"Whatever," Kenzie said, rolling her eyes. "Come on, let's get this meeting over with."

"Fine." Maggie sighed. "But I want to be Mrs. Claus if any of Erin's rehabilitating sports patients are going to play Santa."

During the time Kenzie hid out, Erin decided to look at the buildings Kenzie had recommended and it turned out she liked them. The business was set to open by September. The property offered the privacy that her clients needed.

The pounding of her heart deafened Kenzie. With each step she took the blood in her veins pumped harder. She almost got dizzy and thought she might fall backward. She almost did. Maggie gripped her arm.

"I've got you."

The glass doors opened before either of them touched the brass handles. He kept the handles, she thought. Just from the walk up Kenzie was able to tell Ramon had put in a lot of work to restore the brick.

"Welcome," said a familiar face, with short, tight, curly hair and golden-bronze skin, wrapped in a black tuxedo. "Hi, Kenzie."

"Julio?" Kenzie said slowly. "You're here?"

Julio bowed at the waist and held the door open with his butt. "Temporary situation or penance, however you want to look at it." He extended his hand toward her. "Before you take a step farther, I must apologize to you. I let my greed overtake me when I found out about the building and therefore I placed Ramon's relationship with you at risk."

The apology sounded rehearsed but not forced. "Thank you."

"Right this way," Julio said, stepping aside.

The first thing Kenzie noticed was the floors, still black and white but shiny this time. The postal workers' area was now set up as a baseball-themed bar with bat-and-glove-shaped bar stools. What threw her off for a moment was that there were high school kids in their lettermen jackets sitting at the juice bar where the counter used to be. Kenzie looked around the area further. Pinball machines were surrounded by more teenagers. Beanbag chairs, a popcorn machine and a pool table were farther into the room.

"Is this a rec center?" Maggie asked.

"Right this way," Julio said, not answering Maggie. He led them to the elevator. Kenzie gulped with the memory of the last time she'd been in here. The brass doors to the old-fashioned elevator opened to reveal Raul, also dressed in a tuxedo.

"Good afternoon, Kenzie," Raul said. "Welcome back to Southwood. What brings you here?"

"The Christmas Advisory Council?" Kenzie answered uncertainly. Had no one told him why they were here?

"Ah, yes, I believe it is being held on the second floor."

Okay, now they were getting somewhere. The compartment went up smoothly, no shakes or hiccups. Unlike the noise from the first floor this room remained quiet, even with the dozen students sitting on the couches studying.

Kenzie waved in apology at the students, who looked up from their books.

Raul closed the door. "My bad. I thought the meeting was on the second floor."

Once they reached the third floor the doors opened and once again the area was quiet but still filled with people— older people admiring photographs hanging from the crisp white walls.

"Auntie Bren?" Kenzie asked, stepping off the elevator.

Auntie Bren turned around in her deep purple heels and long purple maxi dress. In one hand she held a glass of red, in the other Oscar's hand. Kenzie's eyes darted to their hands' tender embrace. "I thought you... How long have you been in town?"

"She hasn't left," answered Oscar. He brought Auntie Bren's left hand to his mouth and kissed the back of her hand. "I finally got your aunt to come to her senses."

"Say what?" Maggie hollered. "How long were we gone? Auntie Bren, you told us..."

"I know what I said, girl," Auntie Bren snapped, then quickly recovered. "I know I was set to leave and never return but someone helped me come to realize how much I love him."

Oscar snorted. "You mean Ramon Torres gave you the box from Priscilla's footlocker and you realized she had been keeping my letters to you and not sending yours to me."

"What?" Kenzie and Maggie chorused.

"Oh, sweetheart," Auntie Bren said, "you better get on upstairs to your meeting. You don't want to be late."

"This way," said Raul.

Kenzie's heart began to beat faster. So the first floor was a rec center. The second floor had been turned into a study center; now the third floor was a museum of Southwood artifacts and memorabilia? Tears began to form in her eyes. Blinded, she wiped them away when the doors to the fourth floor opened. Aunt Jody greeted her with a big hug. She smelled more like lilacs than her usual scent of fruity alcohol. Kenzie dabbed the corners of her eyes with her fingertips. Now with the room clearer she spotted her former Tiara Squad members from her generation and more. Felicia, wearing the two-inch runner-up tiara, stepped forward. Was this some form of official dethroning ceremony?

"Kenzie," Felicia said. Lexi waddled to Felicia's side. Waverly flanked Felicia's other side and Bailey brought up the rear with her Miss Southwood tiara. Everyone wore their tiaras. "This is yours," said Felicia. She held out a lavender pillow with gold trimming and Kenzie's old crown perched on top.

"Ramon combed through old photographs of your pageant. He got with the Miss Southwood Organization and discovered the votes were cast by the audience. Everyone received a ballot, just like how prom votes for the prom queen. There were over a hundred people there" said Lexi. "The missing votes weren't enough for you to lose. You're still a Miss Southwood beauty queen."

Felicia threw her arms around Kenzie's neck. "Let's face it, you were always and will always be Miss Southwood."

Someone placed the crown on top of Kenzie's head. The same elation she felt when she received her PhD and shook the chancellor's hand whipped through her. "But I can't take this knowing someone tried to cheat for me. People will always assume I am a cheater."

"No, they won't." Aunt Jody stepped in front of Kenzie. She realized something was missing from the top of her dark head. Kenzie narrowed her eyes but Aunt Jody gave her an assuring smile. "I was in a really competitive stage," she said. "I swapped out some of the votes. I've confessed and I resigned as a Miss Southwood runner-up."

A thousand questions went through Kenzie's mind. But she didn't have a chance to ask any of them. Raul tugged on her elbow.

"Sorry, Kenzie," he said. "I had the wrong floor again. The meeting is in the basement."

Sniffling, Kenzie stepped back on the elevator. Ramon had not only fixed the building like she'd dreamed, but he'd gotten Aunt Bren and Oscar back together, and now he'd restored her tiara.

"Are you okay?" Maggie asked when the elevator doors closed.

"No," Kenzie cried. Her hand shook. "I need to see Ramon."

"I believe he's serving on the committee," Raul answered. "Damn, if only this elevator would stop jamming."

The elevator stalled. Kenzie cursed her luck for always jinxing the things. Finally, after five minutes of tinkering with the buttons and the call service, they began to descend to the basement. Kenzie tried to plan out in her mind what she was going to say to Ramon. She'd spent a month away from him thinking she was over and out of love with him. In a matter of ten minutes and without even seeing him, Kenzie realized she never wanted to be away from him for another minute.

"Here we go."

The doors opened and Kenzie stepped out with quickness, eager to find Ramon. She didn't care who was here for the meeting. She needed him now. She needed to feel him in her arms before she burst.

Jose Torres greeted Kenzie, also in a tuxedo. "Ah, you're here. I bet you're looking for Ramon."

"I am," Kenzie replied, craning her neck.

For the first Christmas Advisory Council meeting, there were a lot of people, enough to stand shoulder to shoulder. Kenzie teetered on her tiptoes to find the top of Ramon's head. No luck. She made her way to the center of the room, spotting her parents first. The Christmas Advisory Council was never a formal event, yet her parents stood out arm in arm, dressed in a cocktail event dress and a tuxedo. No one sat at the tables. There weren't any agendas set out for people to go over. This was not a traditional meeting. As a matter of fact, there was only one chair, in the center of the room, on top of a bunch of magnolia petals.

Jose led Kenzie by the elbow to the center of the room to the chair. "Ramon will be right with you."

For some reason, Kenzie sat. She realized everyone in the room was staring at her. She gulped in anticipation. The group in front of her parted. Ramon appeared, like his brothers, dressed in a black-on-black tuxedo. His hair was cut short. Way short. Tears formed again.

"You're back," Ramon said, approaching.

The last time he'd come toward her, they had not been on the best terms. Kenzie stood to meet him. "You got a haircut."

"Locks for Love." Ramon nodded. "How have you been?"

Kenzie blinked and looked to her left and her right. "Small talk? Can we go someplace private?"

"No," he said, shaking his head. "Are you embarrassed?"

She shrugged. "Maybe."

"Not as embarrassed as I am."

"What do you have to be embarrassed about?" Kenzie asked. She stepped closer and pressed her hand over her heart. "I'm the one who behaved horribly."

"I let you get away from me," said Ramon.

"Looks like you've been busy," Kenzie tried to joke.

"I have. I'm doing everything I can, Kenzie, to ensure you never leave my side again. We're going to have hard times and bumpy times, but I don't want to be like Auntie Bren…" He paused, waiting for her to stop him. She couldn't stop him. After what he'd done for her, he was family. "I don't want any time to pass between us when we fight. And we will argue—it is human nature."

The married couples in the room all agreed with him. Kenzie turned around to see who all found it funny. When she came back to face Ramon, he was kneeling in front of her. "Kenzie, I love you. I don't want to spend one more day without you."

"I love you, too." Kenzie began to weep. Tears rolled down her eyes as Ramon reached into his pocket and extracted a beautiful diamond ring."

"Mackenzie Hairston Swayne, my Dr. Beauty Queen," he said. "Will you do me the honor and please be my wife?"

And for once, without argument or debate, Kenzie said yes.

* * * * *

KIMANI
ROMANCE™

COMING NEXT MONTH
Available June 19, 2018

#577 UNDENIABLE ATTRACTION
Burkes of Sheridan Falls • by Kayla Perrin

When a family wedding reunites Melissa Conwell with Aaron Burke, she's determined to prove she's over the gorgeous soccer star who broke her heart years before. Newly single Aaron wants another chance with Melissa and engineers a full-throttle seduction. Will Melissa risk heartbreak again for an elusive happily-ever-after?

#578 FRENCH QUARTER KISSES
Love in the Big Easy • by Zuri Day

Pierre LeBlanc is a triple threat: celebrated chef, food-network star and owner of the Big Easy's hottest restaurant. Journalist Rosalyn Arnaud sees only a spoiled playboy not worthy of front-page news. Their attraction tells another story. But when she uncovers his secret, their love affair could end in shattering betrayal…

#579 GUARDING HIS HEART
Scoring for Love • by Synithia Williams

Basketball star Kevin Koucky plans to end his career by posing naked in a magazine feature. When photographer Jasmine Hook agrees to take the assignment, she never expects a sensual slam dunk. But he comes with emotional baggage. Little does she know that Kevin always plays to win…

#580 A TASTE OF PLEASURE
Deliciously Dechamps • by Chloe Blake

Italy is the perfect place for new beginnings—that's what chef Danica Nilsson hopes. But one look at Antonio Dante Lorenzetti and her plan to keep romance out of her kitchen goes up in flames. The millionaire restaurateur wants stability. Not unbridled passion. Is she who he's been waiting for?

Get 2 Free Books,
Plus 2 Free Gifts—
just for trying the
Reader Service!

YES! Please send me 2 FREE Harlequin® Kimani™ Romance novels and my 2 FREE gifts (gifts are worth about $10 retail). After receiving them, if I don't wish to receive any more books, I can return the shipping statement marked "cancel." If I don't cancel, I will receive 4 brand-new novels every month and be billed just $5.69 per book in the U.S. or $6.24 per book in Canada. That's a savings of at least 12% off the cover price. It's quite a bargain! Shipping and handling is just 50¢ per book in the U.S. and 75¢ per book in Canada*. I understand that accepting the 2 free books and gifts places me under no obligation to buy anything. I can always return a shipment and cancel at any time. The free books and gifts are mine to keep no matter what I decide.

168/368 XDN GMWW

Name   (PLEASE PRINT)

Address   Apt. #

City   State/Prov.   Zip/Postal Code

Signature (if under 18, a parent or guardian must sign)

Mail to the **Reader Service:**
IN U.S.A.: P.O. Box 1341, Buffalo, NY 14240-8531
IN CANADA: P.O. Box 603, Fort Erie, Ontario L2A 5X3

Want to try two free books from another line?
Call 1-800-873-8635 or visit www.ReaderService.com.

*Terms and prices subject to change without notice. Prices do not include applicable taxes. Sales tax applicable in NY. Canadian residents will be charged applicable taxes. Offer not valid in Quebec. This offer is limited to one order per household. Books received may not be as shown. Not valid for current subscribers to Harlequin® Kimani™ Romance books. All orders subject to approval. Credit or debit balances in a customer's account(s) may be offset by any other outstanding balance owed by or to the customer. Please allow 4 to 6 weeks for delivery. Offer available while quantities last.

Your Privacy—The Reader Service is committed to protecting your privacy. Our Privacy Policy is available online at www.ReaderService.com or upon request from the Reader Service.

We make a portion of our mailing list available to reputable third parties that offer products we believe may interest you. If you prefer that we not exchange your name with third parties, or if you wish to clarify or modify your communication preferences, please visit us at www.ReaderService.com/consumerchoice or write to us at Reader Service Preference Service, P.O. Box 9062, Buffalo, NY 14240-9062. Include your complete name and address.

KROM17R3

SPECIAL EXCERPT FROM

*When a family wedding reunites Melissa Conwell
with Aaron Burke, she's determined to prove she's over the
gorgeous soccer star who broke her heart years before.
Newly single Aaron wants another chance with Melissa
and engineers a plan for a full-throttle seduction. Will
Melissa risk heartbreak again for the elusive dream of a
happily-ever-after?*

Read on for a sneak peek at
UNDENIABLE ATTRACTION,
the first exciting installment in author Kayla Perrin's
BURKES OF SHERIDAN FALLS *series!*

"This is certainly going to be one interesting weekend," she muttered.

"It sure is."

A jolt hit Melissa's body with the force of a soccer ball slamming into her chest. That voice… A tingling sensation spread across her shoulder blades. It was a voice she hadn't heard in a long time. Deeper than she remembered, but it most definitely belonged to *him*.

Holding her breath, she turned. And there he was. Aaron Burke. Looking down at her with a smile on his face and a teasing glint in his eyes.

"I thought that was you," he said, his smile deepening.

Melissa stood there looking up at him from wide eyes, unsure what to say. Why was he grinning at her as though he was happy to see her?

"It's good to see you, Melissa."

Aaron spread his arms wide, an invitation. But Melissa stood still, as if paralyzed. With a little chuckle, Aaron stepped forward and wrapped his arms around her.

Melissa's heart pounded wildly. Why was he doing this? Hugging her as if they were old friends? As if he hadn't taken her virginity and then broken her heart.

"So we're paired off for the wedding," Aaron said as he broke the hug.

"So we are," Melissa said tersely. She was surprised that she'd found her voice. Her entire body was taut, her head light. She was mad at herself for having any reaction to this man.

"You're right. It's going to be a very interesting weekend indeed," Aaron said, echoing her earlier comment.

He looked good. More than good. He looked…delectable. Six feet two inches of pure Adonis, his body honed to perfection. Wide shoulders, brawny arms fully visible in his short-sleeved dress shirt and a muscular chest. His strong upper body tapered to a narrow waist. A wave of heat flowed through Melissa's veins, and she swallowed at the uncomfortable sensation. She quickly averted her eyes from his body and took a sip of champagne, trying to ignore the warmth pulsing inside.

Good grief, what was wrong with her? She should be immune to Aaron's good looks. And yet she couldn't deny the visceral response that had shot through her body at seeing him again.

It was simply the reaction of a female toward a man who was amazingly gorgeous. She wasn't dead, after all. She could find him physically attractive even if she despised him.

Although *despised* was too strong a word. He didn't matter to her enough for her to despise him.

Still, she couldn't help giving him another surreptitious once-over. He had filled out—everywhere. His arms were bigger, his shoulders wider, his legs more muscular. His lips were full and surrounded by a thin goatee—and good Lord, did they ever look kissable…

Don't miss UNDENIABLE ATTRACTION
by Kayla Perrin, available July 2018
wherever Harlequin® Kimani Romance™
books and ebooks are sold.